More Praise for
A Small Thing to Want

These are stories so good you won't want them to end, but when they do, filled with rich characters and wonderful technical gambits, they always satisfy and resonate. An excellent collection.

—Fred Leebron, author of *In the Middle of All This*

Despite the book's title, the desires of the characters in Shuly Cawood's collection, *A Small Thing to Want*, are anything but small. These twelve stories are grounded in domestic detail, but in the vein of Anne Tyler or Elizabeth Strout, each gesture reveals a world of longing: for self-knowledge, for connection, for clarity. At times sad, often wryly funny, always deeply empathetic, Cawood's prose elevates her subjects beyond their everyday circumstances.

—Kate Geiselman, editor of *Flights* literary magazine

Shuly Cawood's writing style is clean, fresh, as she explores the messiness of marital relationships. Compelling stories deliver characters in crisis, certain to engage readers in each unpredictable outcome. High praise for this strong, clever collection.

—Evan Williams, author of *Ripples*

Shuly Cawood's stories are inhabited by lovely and loving characters, people who wander the maze of human relationships, sometimes finding their way, often getting sidetracked, always living to search for love another day. A sure and beautiful writing style tells us there is more boiling beneath the surface than we will ever know.

—Barry Kitterman, editor of *Zone 3*

A
SMALL
THING
TO
WANT

STORIES

Shuly Xóchitl Cawood

Press 53
Winston-Salem

Press 53, LLC
PO Box 30314
Winston-Salem, NC 27130

First Edition

Cover design by Claire V. Foxx

Cover art, "Valentine's," Copyright © 2013 by AskinTulayOver,
licensed through iStock

Library of Congress Control Number
2019956051

Printed on acid-free paper
ISBN 978-1-950413-17-1

To my parents, Sonia and Hap Cawood,
the brightest stars in my every sky

The author thanks the editors of the following publications where these stories first appeared.

Flights, 2017: "Found & Lost"

Jabberwock Review, January 2019: "Good Enough"

The Maine Review, Fall 2017: "Happy" (as "Several States Away")

New Madrid Journal, Summer 2018: "Bag of Boots"

Platypus Press, October 2018: "Trying to Grow"

Prime Number Magazine, Isssue 173, April 2020: "Hank's Girl"

Zone 3, November 2016: "The Snowstorm"

Contents

GOOD ENOUGH

Alice Barrington's hands are small, her fingers thin, but in gloves they look thick and strong—borrowed hands, she thinks—and it is with these hands that she digs a hole two feet deep, pries the redbud tree from its black plastic pot, cuts the roots with her spade and settles it into the hole, a hole she will fill with dirt, old dirt and new dirt mixed together because that's how it works, the only way that one day the leaves will flare green and soak in sun.

Alice presses the dirt against the redbud's small neck of a trunk. Her mother once told her that a bare neckline meant a woman was asking for trouble. Alice wipes the sweat from her forehead with her sleeve.

Striding up to the fence line is Alice's new neighbor—new because Alice just moved in days ago with her two young daughters. The new neighbor has a broad chest and thick arms and legs, and he is frowning as he walks toward her, as if he doesn't know how to do anything but frown, and he is much taller than Alice, who seems shorter now than she was even months ago, though she is just thirty-two years old. The new neighbor has hair that reminds Alice of a tiger, dark brown with blonde streaks, hit by a sun that forgives no one. He tells her his name is Dale, asks if she needs help planting the tree, but of course now she has finished, sweat dripping like tears down her neck and soaking into her shirt.

"I'm fine," she tells him, the same thing she is always telling everyone though it's hardly true. "But thank you," she says, remembering to be polite even though she isn't introducing herself as she picks up her shovel and moves toward the shed and away from him, before she breaks wide open.

Dale watches his new neighbor from his screened-in back porch. He's been watching her for the last half hour as she digs. A pitiful redbud sapling in a black plastic pot awaits. His new neighbor's backyard and Dale's backyard are divided by a rustic split fence Dale installed himself several summers ago. Perfect for a big dog, more than one neighbor has told him over the years, but Dale didn't install the fence because he wants a dog. He wants to know what is his.

The neighbor is shoveling but in tiny scoops. She needs to pierce the ground with the shovel's end. He wants to help her but doesn't want to offend her. Dale's last girlfriend accused him of always trying to get her to do things his way. He doesn't need to have his way; he just likes to see things done the right way, and he hates inefficiencies, hates them the way he hates screaming babies on a plane and people who don't fess up to their mistakes, which his ex-girlfriend could write a book about if she knew how to put an honest sentence together. When they broke up, she said Dale always let everyone go eventually, but that's not true. Part of him couldn't stand the space the girlfriend took up, like air sucked from his own lungs. He's waiting for the one who will be different, who will provide oxygen instead of drawing it away.

Watching his new neighbor makes his hands tingle, as if they might go numb, which maybe they will if he doesn't keep opening and closing them. His neck, the back of it, burns—like a stovetop, like sand on a beach at noon under the glare of day, like an all-or-nothing bet he's lost already. Forget the ex-girlfriend, what does she know anyway. Dale opens the porch door, sits on the stoop and pulls on his work boots, laces them over the flecks of mud, and moves toward his new neighbor across the lawn he has mowed so meticulously a person could run a hand over it and the blades would all stand at the same height, all reaching simultaneously for something they are incapable of seeing but still understand.

"She's a widow," Chloe Livioni tells Dale in a hushed tone one morning. Chloe lives six houses away, and she has stopped to talk with Dale, as she often does if he happens to be out in his front yard as she trots by with her standard poodle. Several of the neighbor ladies take it upon themselves to stop and chat with him whenever he works outside—especially when he forgoes a T-shirt, which he tries not to do, particularly in the front yard.

Chloe is single and an "artist," whatever that means—Dale only knows she doesn't seem to have anything to do, and she talks about muses and evoking inspiration, and her fingers are perpetually smudged with ink. In the summers, Chloe keeps her hair in two short braids and wears white cotton tank tops with no bra, and white billowy cotton skirts, and black underwear that shadows below the folds of her skirt. She usually talks for too long, but today Dale stops spreading mulch and listens: *Alice Barrington, two daughters, one eight years old and the other five.* He's seen them, blonde and petite and beautiful, like their mother.

"His name was Jack," Chloe confides.

"Whose name?"

"The husband," she says. Chloe has a high-pitched voice that makes Dale think of the sounds only dogs can hear. "Do you want to know how he died?" she asks.

"I've got to get back to it," Dale says, hauling upright a bag of mulch and tearing its top open.

Chloe Livioni is having a potluck party, and though Dale hates Chloe's parties—notorious for being filled with pot smoke and liberals—Chloe mentions one morning that she has invited everyone in the neighborhood, including Alice Barrington.

The night of the party, Dale paces in his living room, back and forth, back and forth. He waits until it's an hour into the party before going over, refusing to be the first to arrive. He did that one year, so used to being punctual, and Chloe wrangled him into grilling skewers of onions and mushrooms and chunks of zucchini almost the entire evening, which he would not have minded, as he likes having a purpose, but she appointed herself his assistant and yammered at him the whole time and at one point asked didn't they make a great team, and he knew better than to answer. Tonight he brings a six-pack of pale ale beer and some hummus he made himself with a kick of extra lime and a few dollops more of tahini—he likes the bitterness of it—along with a bag of fresh pita. By the time he arrives, Dale is already sweating a little, in the middle of his back, though the evening has turned out to be cool. Guests are packed into Chloe's living room, they are laughing and chatting it up, and in one corner, a group of musicians—there is always this group at Chloe's—sits around in a circle in folding chairs, screeching out bluegrass tunes with fiddles and an assortment of other instruments, none of which Dale can name. Off the living room, the sliding glass door that leads to the backyard is wide open, screen door be damned, and people mill in and out of the house freely. Dale spots Chloe in the kitchen congested with friends and neighbors, a few of whom greet him. Sometimes he hates living in this Ohio village, all talk and gossip and small-town politics, but tonight he is grateful for a few friendly faces.

"You made it!" Chloe calls out, waving from across the kitchen, and he nods and sets his offerings on the table, grabs two beers and heads back into the living room and out the sliding glass door onto the enormous deck that wraps around the side of the house, too. Strings of lights hang all across the back of the house, and citronella torches everywhere burn the evening air. A few people are sitting around a fire pit in the middle of the yard, but no Alice Barrington, just faces of people he has talked to in past years, people who have talked to him, some of whom remember things about him: that he's a civil engineer and a Luddite, that he's from Idaho, and that he once made two Adirondack chairs just to see if he could. He glances at someone sitting on the edge of the deck alone, and there is Alice in a white blouse and yellow pants, sandals kicked off, her feet hiding in the grass.

"Hey," he says, going to her. Alice looks up, her eyes red. Has she been crying? "Lost?" he asks. "You know the party's in there," he says, thumbing toward the kitchen, although he's relieved she is by herself.

"I got a little overwhelmed," Alice says. Her face contains a dusting of freckles, dots on a treasure map. "I came out for some fresh air."

"Beer?" He holds up the second bottle.

"Thank God and yes, please," she says and gives him just enough of a smile to keep him from leaving. Her two front teeth are slightly crooked, the perfect amount to be charming. "I didn't want to go back in there just yet."

He fishes a bottle opener from his pocket and snaps off the cap, hands the beer over.

"Are people eating dessert yet?" she asks. "Dale, right? I'm sorry I didn't introduce myself the other day."

"May I?"

She nods and scoots over, and he sits on the edge of the deck, too, near her but not right beside her.

"I was rude the other day," she says.

He snaps off the cap of his beer but doesn't drink any yet. "You were fine."

"*Fine,*" she says. "Such an optimistic word."

"It's your first Chloe party." He clinks his beer bottle against hers but only takes a sip. "Always good to bring some optimism to one of these." He's thirsty but also nervous, and he knows when he's nervous his hands fumble. He sets the beer down and leans back on his arms, his palms flat against the deck floor. Bluegrass music swells from inside the house and out into the yard.

"I haven't been to a party in a long time," she says. "I'm not usually a big-party person, but Chloe got her niece to babysit for me, which was so nice, and I just needed to get out of the house, to have a few moments. Today was just one of those days." Blonde strands have escaped the elastic band with which she has tied back her hair. "Do you ever just need a break from your regularly scheduled life?"

"Of course."

"You live alone, right? I mean, I only know that because Chloe told me."

"Were you asking about me?"

She blushes. "Oh, I would never—"

"I'm kidding," he says. He was, mostly. "Don't listen to what Chloe says about me anyway, although she got that part right."

"Aren't you and Chloe friends?"

One time, a couple of years ago, Chloe called him late at night to come over because she said she heard noises in the basement. Dale rushed to her house only to find Chloe drunk, hair tousled, sprawled atop the kitchen counter waiting for him, wearing the same summer tank top she always wore with no bra, but this time she wasn't wearing a skirt, either, just the pair of black panties. "We're neighbors," Dale says. "We get along."

"She said you liked your alone time."

"Sometimes," he says. Less and less, really.

"I don't know if I like alone time." She rubs the back of her neck. "I used to love it, and now I rarely get it, and when I do, it's . . . challenging." A citronella torch fizzles. "Maybe I'm just tired of thinking."

"Thinking is overrated." He picks up the beer and takes another sip and stretches out his legs. Then he remembers that his last girlfriend accused him of being too self-centered, never thinking of anyone but himself. "Where do you work?"

"The art museum—I help with marketing and brand management. It doesn't pay great, but the benefits are good and the hours are flexible, so I can work from home when I need to. Jack—my husband—got me the job. Jack is," her voice falters, "Jack was—"

"I heard," Dale says, saving her, saving himself, he doesn't know which.

"You heard he was an extrovert?"

"No, I heard. . . . Sorry," he says. "Chloe said some things."

"Oh yes, Chloe. Well, word does get around."

Is he supposed to ask about Jack? He doesn't want to. In fact Jack is the last thing he wants to talk about. "I saw your girls with a black cat."

"You did? Do you know whose cat he is?"

"There are tons of strays in the neighborhood," Dale says. "I'm sure it's just another one. You can keep it, if that's what you're wondering."

"Oh God no. I can't handle a cat. I was hoping you knew where he belonged. The girls have named him: Wibbles. Wibbles! I know I should take him to the pound before they get too attached."

"Best not to get attached."

"The girls love that cat."

"They'll be fine without it."

"I don't have the energy right now for another thing, but I haven't had the heart to take him away from them," Alice says. "They've lost so much already. But I can't manage a cat. Do you ever know something, but you don't want to face it? I feel like my whole life is like that right now." Alice takes a drink and then sets the bottle next to her, as if she might be done. "I'm sorry. I don't know why I'm telling you all this. I think all this beer has gotten to my head."

"How many have you had?"

"I don't usually talk this much. I used to be able to contain everything but ever since—"

"I'll take the cat," Dale says.

"What?"

"I'll take it, pay for everything, manage it all." How hard can a cat be? "The girls can come over any time they want to play with . . . Wibbles, is that its name?"

"Are you being serious?"

"Funny name for a cat. Funny name for anything."

"Did you want a cat?"

"I wanted a cook. I'm assuming the cat can cook?"

She laughs, and his stomach tumbles. He should have eaten. He hasn't eaten. He is so hungry now.

The bluegrass group has taken a break, so the cicadas can be heard now, their rattles in rhythms, rising and falling. Fireflies pulse their light into the darkening day, and a breeze shifts the leaves in the trees.

"I can't thank you enough," she says, pushing back the stray strands of hair from her face. "Really."

"It's nothing."

Stars peer from behind clouds slipping across the sky. A quiet settles between Dale and Alice, a peace, and he breathes it in.

The bluegrass group starts up again with another fiddle tune, but now there must be more musicians, or fewer, or better ones because the tune has a new and kinder cadence, as if the music is asking and answering.

And then: "Hey!" It's Chloe and her high-pitched voice, coming toward them. "There you are." She stands over them, hands on her hips. "What are you doing out here? You should come in and eat. Have you eaten?"

"We're good." Dale raises his beer bottle like he is making a toast.

"Well, I think you should eat."

"Chloe!" A woman steps out onto the deck. "Where's your mop?"

"Wait one minute," Chloe says to them, holding up a pointer finger, "I'll be right back," before rushing into the house.

Dale and Alice look at each other and laugh. Another breeze shifts their way, one that might carry rain in the distance but now carries the scent of knockout roses in their second blooming, the smell of love and funerals.

Alice reaches out and catches a firefly in her cupped hand. "Chloe wants to set me up next week," she says. "Everyone keeps telling me it's time to start again." Alice lifts her hand in the air, and the firefly lifts, also, into darkness. "He's an English professor."

"Sounds boring." Dale doesn't want to know more. "Don't let Chloe set you up."

"She says he's very nice."

"Nice is a four-letter word. Sort of like *fine*."

"Maybe. But maybe nice is what I need now."

"Maybe what you need is some good dessert." He stands. "Shall we?" He holds out his hand, and she puts hers in his, and he helps lift her to her feet. He walks behind her into the kitchen and will not leave her side all night, will make sure she has everything she needs—extra napkins, a glass of ice water, a spoon for the ice cream melted over apple cobbler—and Dale will stay later than he has ever stayed at any neighborhood party before, or will again.

The engine of the black cat's purring soothes Dale, the fur softening the edges of long days. When Dale stands at the sink shaving, he lets the cat wander between his legs, and as he watches television, the cat brushes up against him, settling onto his feet. Eventually, Wibbles leaps up one night and sleeps on the lonesome extra pillow Dale keeps on his king bed.

Dale is diligent, bringing Wibbles over to the fence line, placing the cat into the outstretched arms of Alice's two girls, telling them to take him for the day, bring him back that night. Sometimes Alice walks with the girls around the block to arrive at Dale's front door to return Wibbles. Dale tries to invite them in for dinner—steaks he's already made, potatoes he has buttered and wrapped in foil—but the girls and Alice never stay.

"It's time for the girls to go to bed," Alice says.

So put them to bed, he wants to say.

"But thank you," Alice always adds. "Really. It means a lot to the girls. Say thank you, girls."

A chorus of thank yous rises to Dale like a song, but the song ends there.

After a while, Alice sends the girls over alone to knock on his door, or if Dale happens to be working in his yard, which he often does, she sends the girls to the fence line to hand Wibbles over at dusk. Alice stands on her deck watching them, waiting for them to go and return before heading inside. She waves at Dale when the handing over is done, and it always seems as if Alice is standing on the back of a ship that is drifting away.

"Bob Anderson is fabulous for her. I made a perfect match," Chloe says, stroking the standard poodle's head as Dale rakes the first falling of leaves, not stopping to talk to Chloe. The rake scratches the lawn clean of shredded leaves.

Chloe shouldn't assume he knows who the hell Bob is, and he wants to ask, "Who the hell is Bob?" but he knows: Bob, a college professor in English. Bob with his brown station wagon. Bob Anderson with his wire-rimmed glasses and skinny arms and legs. Dale has seen him, more than once.

"Have you seen them together?" Chloe asks.

"Don't think so." Dale rakes harder.

"If you did, you'd remember. They look so happy."

Chloe's poodle squats and pees in Dale's yard.

"Good do-your-business," Chloe says to the dog and fishes a treat from her skirt pocket and hands it to the poodle. "I'll have to have you and them over," she says to Dale.

"Please don't let your dog crap on my lawn," he says.

"She knows better. Don't you, girl?"

The poodle wags its tail.

It's mid-November, and the chill finds its way into every room in Dale's house, every corner and crevice. Bob's station wagon is always lingering at Alice's now, in the driveway, on the street. Dale drives by on his way to and from work, a block out of the way, but he faces forward, clutching his steering wheel, catching—out of the corner of his eye—pink, sparkly stickers stuck to the back seat windows of Bob's old brown car.

The week before Thanksgiving, the woman who always cuts Dale's hair at Quick Clips asks if she can give his phone number to her friend. "I think you'll really hit it off," she says, her long beaded earrings swinging back and forth as if they don't know which way to go.

Antonia pulls into the parking lot of Linardos to meet Dale on a blind date, the day after Thanksgiving. Her girlfriend cuts his hair, always the same style: the Side Part. Antonia's girlfriend swears Dale's in a rut and needs a change. Antonia's the one who called Dale, asked him for dinner, and he seemed reluctant—he pushed off the date once, claimed he had to work late—but when she finds him at a table by the window, and as they make small talk and order, as he pours her wine from a bottle he chose and offers her bread from the basket before taking some himself, Antonia thinks about how Dale is exactly as her girlfriend described: distant but attentive, soft-spoken but blunt. Antonia asks him what he thinks of the place she picked—it's her favorite (though she doesn't admit this)—and he says he's been to restaurants that make a much better braciolone but the ambience of the place is pretty good, "old school," he calls it with an approving nod, a man who must like tradition. He lets her do all the talking, which her last boyfriend never let her do, always needing to hog the floor, and Dale walks her to her car when the date is over, which is more than most men do, and he says he'll call, and though it isn't for another week, he calls, and that's what matters.

Bob's moving in with Alice, Chloe announces when Dale runs into her at the grocery store. "Here Comes Santa Claus" plays on the speakers, the Muzak version, the kind Dale hates. The store's linoleum floors are dirty and wet from the slush of winter boots.

"What are you buying?" Chloe peers into his grocery cart. "Wine? Cheese and crackers? Is there something I should know?"

Antonia has long brunette hair that sweeps across her back, straight as if it's been ironed carefully. She wears dark red lipstick, the color of crushed pomegranate. Even when she and Dale kiss, the color doesn't come off, but later, after the first time they have sex—in her house, in her bed—after he rises, readies to leave in the gray morning hour before work, after Antonia rises, too, hurrying off to the kitchen to make him coffee before he hits the road, Dale finds smears of red lipstick across the pillowcases, as if he has cut Antonia open and caused her to lose something vital, something she won't be able to get back, no matter how hard he tries.

One winter Saturday, when there is a break from ice and snow, Dale and Antonia drive to the Newport Aquarium across the river from Cincinnati: Antonia wants to see the penguins. They stand at the glass and gaze at the black-and-white creatures waddling on rock and snow, plunging into water, bellies like buoys.

Antonia taps on the glass, even though signs everywhere say explicitly not to. Dale almost tells her to stop. The room feels stuffed with heat and oniony body odor and kids yanking on their parents' sleeves. Dale sits on a bench as Antonia tries to connect with a world from which she is separated, a world she cannot touch, can never really know.

"You ready to go?" he finally says, less like a question than a demand.

"Not yet," Antonia says. "We just got here."

♦ ♦ ♦

The redbud blooms just over Alice's side of the fence: magenta blossoms thrusting open.

Antonia has begun to raise her voice when she and Dale argue. The more he keeps silent, the louder Antonia becomes. Her face looks like a hot tomato when she tries to make her points, or just before she slams a door or two. Dale reads the newspaper, the same paragraph over and over. He remains still, as if stillness equated invisibility, a myth he believed in as a kid in a house clouded with anger. Dale and Antonia fight about—more than any other thing—Wibbles. Antonia is allergic to cats, she sneezes when too long in the same room, her eyes water as if she were crying. She's asked Dale, she's begged Dale, to please get rid of the cat. Let's just see how it goes, he tells her, though in truth he knows Wibbles is staying. Dale agrees to keep the cat contained to only certain parts of the house, of course not the bedroom, and promises to make Wibbles a mostly outside cat. But there is Wibbles, shivering on the porch, or perched on the outside windowsill, his yellow eyes blinking in at them. In a matter of weeks after Antonia begins spending the night more and more, pushing aside Dale's stack of neatly pressed T-shirts to make some space in a drawer for panties and bras, Wibbles ends up back in the bedroom, first on the floor, then on a chair, and finally on Dale's side of the bed, burrowed between the pillow and headboard, but not the other side.

Isn't that good enough?

Dale talks Antonia into trying, just for a while, some allergy pills, which Antonia begins swallowing every morning and will do for so long she'll lose track of when she began. She'll also start swallowing antidepressants she keeps in unmarked bottles on the nightstand on her side of the bed, a nightstand she claims as best she can with a compact powder and Mary Kay hand cream. She will take those pills—the allergy ones and the antidepressants—for years after she and Dale break up, even after she gets married to someone else.

The daylilies blow open in yellow. Everything in Dale's yard blazes too bright, like it could burn down the lawn. And then just as quickly as they have blown open, they have withered, turning brown, disappearing.

◆◆◆

"They're getting married in Alice's backyard," Chloe says, the poodle sniffing Dale's lawn. "Didn't she invite you?"

"Look, Chloe, I don't have time today." Dale is pruning the shrubs in his front yard. It's late to be doing this, already mid-summer.

"What's wrong? You didn't used to be this pissy."

"I just don't need you to tell me everything that everyone is doing." He should have pruned much earlier, weeks and weeks ago.

"I don't tell you everything," Chloe says, tugging on the poodle's leash to make it shorter and tighter. "By even a stretch."

"Okay," he says, his mouth in drought now.

A car passing by on the street beep-beeps at another car shifting out of a driveway.

"You alright?" Chloe asks.

He nods.

"You don't look alright."

He squints up at the sun, as if assessing what it might do. "Water. I need water." He drops the loppers and heads toward the house.

"You really should keep a bottle of Gatorade out here, you know," Chloe calls out to him as he steps into the cool of the house, sinks onto the cool of the tile floor.

The birds awaken before Dale and begin their singing outside the windows, trying to brighten this Saturday morning hour. Dale throws off the sheets, makes his way to the kitchen and coffeepot. As the boiling water hisses and gurgles through the grounds, Dale surveys his living room. Antonia had remarked once that he did not have photographs of anyone around, as most people do, and for the first time, the absence of faces reminds him of snow, so much of it. All these blank walls and only the occasional piece of art—a metal sculpture, an onyx bowl, a canvas of a brown, fallow field. He can't remember what he liked about that last piece of art, so endlessly empty, why he ever thought to purchase it. He drinks his coffee quickly and heads outside.

Bob is kneeling near the fence line. His skinny legs are pale, his shorts too baggy, as if he were swimming in them. Bob has on bright white sneakers that look like they have never met real dirt. He is leaning over, weeding the bed of annuals he put in, petunias and zinnias, such a waste of time.

"Hey, Dale," Bob calls out as Dale approaches the fence, even though they have never officially met before.

"I need this tree moved," Dale says.

"This?" Bob points to the redbud. "Why?"

"It shouldn't be so close to the fence line." Its leaves will ripen by autumn and drift onto his lawn, making more work. The tree is small, but a leaf is a leaf.

Bob looks to the house. "Alice!"

"No," Dale says. "You need to move it."

"I want to see what she wants," Bob says.

"I don't care what she wants."

"Alice!"

A door creaks open, and Alice emerges. Her hair is held back in a high bun over her head, as if about to tumble down, and her freckles are absent, covered in makeup. Alice walks toward them. "Hey, Dale, what's going on here?"

"Dale wants the tree moved."

Alice shades her eyes to look at Dale, sun behind him. "Why?"

His throat feels tight, like a wrench is twisting it shut. He wants to say, "Why the hell did you put it here?" He wants to yell about the leaves. Instead he says, "Just move it is all," before he heads back inside. His chest feels like its wall is being kicked in.

The clear summer evening looks much the same as the night of Chloe Livioni's potluck party, now a year later, now so long ago, but there are no strings of lights, and there is no scent of citronella, no sounds of bluegrass music, only the sound of Alice's back door slamming shut, startling Dale, who is sitting on his back porch. He sets down his beer and nudges Wibbles from his lap. He stands. Alice hurries to the shed, opens it—she never locks it, which always stumps Dale— and reaches inside for a shovel, and soon Alice is at the fence, driving the pointed metal tool into the ground around the redbud.

The kicking in his chest begins again, and Dale doesn't bother with boots this time, there's no time for boots now, not anymore. He walks straight to the fence and steps on the rails and jumps over.

"Stay out of my yard," Alice says, holding a hand up. "I don't need your help."

"I know."

"Go away."

I can't, he wants to say. He grabs the shovel. "Stop."

Alice won't let go of it.

"Please," he says. "You don't have to move the tree."

"You're telling me that now? It's too late."

"It's not too late."

The cicadas rattle like a fistful of maracas. Sweat beads on the tip of Alice's freckled nose. She shakes her head.

"Then let me do it," Dale says. "I know how to do it so the tree will survive. You're digging too close to the roots. Don't you want it to survive?"

Alice releases the shovel, takes a step back.

"Don't stay out here," he tells her. "Just tell me where you want it. I'll take care of it." He wants her to trust him to do it. She looks at him with narrowed eyes. Finally, her shoulders drop. "Over here," she says, and he follows her, staying back far enough from her heels so he does not step on her.

She points to a spot as far from his property as possible. "Here," she says. "Is this good enough?"

Dale is shoveling now, digging deep and fast. Alice steps away from him, but he can feel her gaze boring into him. He is freezing inside, a cold taking over, despite the sweat climbing out of his pores. He digs far down, hitting rocks now and again. He takes those out, too, chunks of limestone, making sure the tree has room enough to grow, to breathe, to spread its roots and begin again.

Alice stands at her back window, lights off, though Dale can probably see her if he looks over, which he does not do. When the digging is over—the old spot and the new, the redbud sunk into the ground—Dale pats the soil with his thick hands. She had almost offered him some garden gloves but then decided not to.

Dale lengthens the garden hose Alice keeps coiled like a snake by her house, and he squeaks on the faucet and begins the watering, though dusk is nearly done. Alice knows he will stand there and wait until it's over, until it's enough, which will surely be after nightfall. She flicks on her back porch lights so he can see, and when they flash on, Dale blinks up at them before keeping on with the wait.

Dale seems smaller than she remembers thinking he was the night of Chloe Livioni's potluck party, when she and Dale had talked out on Chloe's deck, the fireflies lighting the night in ways that promised magic, movement. For a while, sitting out on Chloe's deck that night, beer idling through Alice's system, she had felt loosened and wonderful.

Alice had let Dale walk her home after the party, let him stand with her at the front door as she fumbled for her key in her pocket, let him touch her face and lift it, let him slip the elastic band off and put his hand through her hair. He had looked at her with such longing, a longing she understood because she felt it, too, for there was an emptiness in each of them that could never be filled. She had closed her eyes and pretended to be someone else, someone for whom there was room for joy, and she had let him kiss her, let him press against her under her porch light that buzzed and flickered, that would need to be fixed, that she had no idea how to fix. Dale let go before Alice wanted him to, but her daughters were asleep inside, and she had a blind date with a nice man in just a few days, a man Chloe Livioni swore was happy and easy, and her husband had killed himself exactly one year ago to the day, to that night, and what else could she do but kiss someone who understood all of it? What else could she do but break away?

BAG OF BOOTS

Miguel's mother, Samoya, is drinking too much at our winter solstice party. She keeps sliding down into the couch, as if she were slipping from the earth. Her eyes close during conversations.

I nudge Miguel. "Go help her."

"Samoya's a big girl. She can handle herself," he says.

"Clearly she can't."

"Let her have some fun," he says. "She's entitled." What he means is *he's* entitled. His father left Samoya nine months ago, on the first day of spring, and Miguel has gone over to her house pretty much every night since then to check on her. To screw in a loose lightbulb. To fix a fuse. To hold her while she sobs. To clean the lint out of the dryer because she says she can't pull out the six-by-four-inch filter.

"Fine," I say. "But I'm not going to stand here and watch."

"So don't," he says. "There are plenty of other rooms in the house." He didn't used to talk to me this way. I suppose I didn't talk to him like this, either.

Eventually Miguel is the one who stalks out of the living room and into the kitchen. I'm the one who stays.

Last year, Miguel re-enrolled in school, finally working on that bachelor's degree he never finished a decade ago. I told him he had to be able to take care of himself. He dropped out because his mother got cancer, the worst kind: ovarian. How Samoya survived I don't know. I think Miguel's father was hoping she wouldn't, but he's too kind to ever admit such a thought. Or too smart to say it out loud. Roy isn't a mean person. He just wanted his freedom, and it seemed easier to do it that way than to let Samoya down. You don't want to let Samoya down if you don't have to because she never forgets it if you do.

It took Roy another seven years after she'd recovered to leave. Maybe he wanted to be sure she would be all right once he did. He restocked the wood for the fireplace though it wasn't the season to do so. He changed the oil in her car the week before, and he planted the spinach and radish seeds in the garden.

Miguel says leaving is leaving, but I disagree.

I wish I could be all the way on Samoya's side about this, the way she wants me to be, the way she needs me and everyone else to be, but I knew Roy first. We worked together years ago when I was just an intern right out of college. Roy was the supervisor you went to if you wanted calm and fair. He was the one who made sure you were heard and seen, and the one who made you believe you could do better, could want more, get more, be more. Roy is why I looked forward to work in the first place, why I showed up a little earlier, stayed a little later, which pissed off the man I was seeing at the time, a man I would eventually give in and marry and, too many years later, divorce. Anyway, Roy is the one, not Samoya, who has that deep belly laugh, who asks me how I'm doing and doesn't say a word until I answer—doesn't interrupt me or glance away like other people do. He's the one who likes to sit on porches and watch thunderstorms roll in, who refuses to buy new when used is more than fine, who doesn't fear tomorrow because it will have a perfectly good sunrise and sunset, even if clouds cover them. Just knowing they are there is a good enough reason to sit back with a cold beer and watch the sky moisten with darkness.

I don't know why Samoya stopped loving him, only that she did. Ever since I've known her, all she's had for him is a bag full of *why can't you* and *why do you always* and *for goodness' sake.* Of course Samoya would say she loved Roy with her whole heart, that she loved him up until the day before he left, that she loved him even on the day she found his collection of boots stashed inside a duffle bag, zipped and ready to be tossed in the truck. She pretended not to know what a bag of boots meant. And who can blame her. We all pretend—the only difference is how much, and when.

Outside our bay window, snow whisks through the branches of the elm tree barren of leaves. Cold laces the pane. Someone has cranked up the radio in the living room, an oldies pop station. "I Heard It through the Grapevine" crackles out of the lone speaker, and people strut around the couch and chairs, beer bottles held high, reenacting *The Big Chill*. These are my friends, of course, who can actually remember the 1980s. I wonder if Miguel even knows what they are doing.

Miguel is thirteen years younger than I am, but his friends are even younger now that he's back in college. This party feels half adult, half frat, with two guys standing in the corner throwing chips up in the air and trying to catch them with their mouths.

When we moved in together two years ago, I told myself it would be temporary, to help him get his feet on the ground after he quit yet another job. Miguel's most valued possessions were his grandfather's turquoise ring, a box of records, and a guitar. Samoya reclaimed the ring; the records, left in his trunk through three seasons, had warped from too much heat and cold. The guitar lies in its coffin of a case shoved beneath the bed. Sometimes I wish Miguel played music the way he used to, the way Roy taught him to, the way a man who knows what he is doing can break a handful of chords in half and put them back together again, make them sound like new.

Samoya is curled up on one end of the couch, asleep, though there are plenty of guests still milling about. They ignore her. She is a throw pillow now, albeit a big one, and they shift her this way and that to make room for themselves.

My coworker, Tommy Erickson, sidles up to me. "Great party," he says. He is wearing a pink Izod polo with the collar turned up. Tommy Erickson never wears long sleeves, even in the dead of winter. He's swirling bourbon in a glass, and the ice clinks against the sides. "I love what you've done to the place."

"Miguel and I did it," I say.

"But you picked the colors, right?" he asks.

"Yes, I suppose I did."

Tommy Erickson smells like a handful of pine needles. "All the dark chocolate and charcoal grays," he says. "Totally you."

"What makes you say that?"

"Oh, please," Tommy Erickson says.

A newly arrived guest slips off her wet shoes. She brushes snow from the front of her brown wool skirt.

Roy told me Samoya saved his life once, when they were dating. He had taken her to play pool—Samoya used to be so good at it then, Roy said, she even had her own cue stick—and they had stayed well into the evening, and by the time they stumbled out of the pool hall, Roy was drunk, as was Samoya, but he less so. He got behind the wheel. He tried to focus, he really did, he said, and I believed him, but the alcohol rendered the road senseless. The grip of the steering wheel felt rubbery and alive. The windshield looked like it was waving. Samoya was laughing in the passenger seat, laughing about who they had beaten in the pool hall: two men who had been sure that no young woman as beautiful as Samoya could, for she was even more beautiful then, like a goddess with her thick and long black hair, those huge green eyes, the high cheekbones, that almond skin that looked as if it had been smoothed from ancient sand, that young and beautiful woman who could make you believe that wishes, any kind, but especially your kind, were what she made come true. Those two men— one with a red bandana wrapped around his head, the other with bits of peanuts that kept getting stuck in his beard—what did they know? How could they have possibly seen what was coming? Her smile and easy small talk. Her hair, swishing like a serpent.

"I can't believe we beat them," Roy said in the car, blinking to try and focus.

"I can." Samoya was laughing again.

And then the deer was there, flashed in the headlights, eyes caught like a hooked fish.

Samoya grabbed the wheel, spun the world, twisted them off the country road, made them miss everything that might have happened.

"Where did you end up?" I asked the first time Roy told me the story. In a ditch? Slammed into a tree?

"Married," Roy said.

Miguel calls to me from down the hallway, which is half dark with its row of shut doors, each like a face rid of emotion. The only light wanders from the living room. When I get to Miguel, who is standing outside the bathroom, he points to the door. I lean in to listen. Someone is throwing up in there.

"Who do you think it is?" I whisper.

"Not my mother," he whispers back.

The retching stops. Our eyes lock. I tap on the door. "You okay in there?"

No answer.

I knock louder. "Hello?" I try the doorknob, but it won't turn.

From the kitchen, the sound of something breaking comes to us. "Go ahead," I say to Miguel. "I can take care of this." Miguel hustles toward the sound, his figure moving down the hallway and toward the light.

Miguel gets itchy when he has to tell Samoya a lie. He starts twitching and shifting from right to left foot and scratching at his sleeves and chest. His neck flares red.

"It'll be better this way," I said just before he told Samoya we were heading to a one-room cabin on Coon County Lake for a mini vacation. We were actually driving an hour and a half away to see Roy, who had rented an apartment above a laundromat in a small town. He wanted to show us the place, have us stay over.

"Which cabin?" Samoya had asked.

"What do you mean?" Miguel rubbed his neck.

"What's the address?" Her voice rose into the sky like a balloon that had lost its string. "What's the phone number there?"

Miguel elbowed me.

"You have our cell phones," I said. "You can reach us anytime."

"Everyone knows there's no cell service in Coon County," Samoya said. "How long will you be gone?"

In the end, we went nowhere. Miguel said he was too tired. He flopped onto our bed without taking off his shoes.

"Roy needs you, too," I said. Our bedside lamp threw meager light into the room.

"You mean he needs me to make her better so she'll give him the divorce."

"He never asked you to do anything," I said. "He told you to stay out of it."

"She's my mom. I'm not gonna let her die."

"Who said anything about dying?"

◆◆◆

The bathroom door clicks open, and a young woman in a brown wool skirt is standing there.

"Hey," I say.

She jumps back. "I didn't see you there."

"You okay?"

She steps into the hallway. "Who are you?"

"Did you drink too much?"

She shakes her head, bites her lower lip, draws her arm across her waist.

"Are you even of age?" I ask.

"Who are you again?"

"Who are *you*?"

"I go to Lehman College with Miguel," she says. She has the kind of makeup that glitters, except you can't see the glitter until you are up close. "And *you*?" she asks.

"This is my house."

"It is?" she says. "I thought this was Miguel's place."

"It is."

"Oh." She opens her mouth, closes it, a camera shutter figuring out the necessary exposure. "Oh."

A few days after that time we didn't go see Roy, I took the afternoon off work and drove to Roy's apartment over the laundromat. I did not tell Miguel. Roy said he would make me my favorite dish of his, egg noodles and cream, and I knew he would burn it just a little because I like it that way. "It's carcinogenic," Miguel always says when I eat it like that. But life is carcinogenic. Roy and I both understand that.

Clanking and muffled conversation rose from below as Roy gave me the tour of his apartment: living room/kitchen with fluorescent fixtures, black-and-white bathroom with chipped subway tile, and the closet-sized bedroom with a skylight.

"Sometimes you can see the moon," he said.

His T-shirt was wrinkled. He smelled like cedar.

"Are you okay?" I asked.

Roy leaned against the bedroom's doorframe. "Loneliness has its place. How about you?"

On the nightstand, a candle; on the bed, two plumped pillows. A blue quilt, looking worn enough to smell of secrets, hung off the edges of the bed.

The skylight promised the moon.

I met Miguel long after Roy and I stopped working together. Miguel was playing soccer with his buddies in one of the fields near where I was playing softball with my coworkers against another office team. Afterward, we all ended up at a bar two blocks away sharing tables and pitchers and nachos and numbers. I was newly divorced and ready for some fun. Tommy Erickson flirted with the redheaded catcher from the other office team, trying to get her to sit on his lap.

Miguel leaned over to me. "What position does that guy play?"

"All of them," I answered, "if we let him."

I didn't know Miguel was Roy's son until three dates later. By that time Miguel and I had slept together. I'd like to think I wouldn't have done that, or even said yes to a date, if I had known to whom Miguel belonged. But maybe I would have. Maybe I wouldn't have given up a thing.

After I flush the toilet a couple of times and light a match to burn off the vomit smell, I leave the bathroom with the fan turned on. Back in the living room, Samoya is awake again but still on the couch, sitting next to Tommy Erickson, who has his arm thrown around her. She is curled into his side, batting her huge green eyes at him. Roy used to talk about how he fell in love with Samoya because her eyes were magical. Tommy Erickson bathes in her gaze. He has a hand in her hair, and he is combing it with his fingers, untangling the long silver and black strands from one another. She murmurs something, and he nods. He twists strands of her hair around his hand like a bandage. That's how long it is: this night, her hair.

Miguel comes up to me. "Go tell him to stop."

"Why should I?"

"He's your friend."

"My coworker," I say.

"Why do you always invite him?"

"Because he makes things interesting."

Samoya motions for Tommy Erickson to hand over his glass, and when he does, she takes a long drink from it, hands it back empty.

I say to Miguel, "Let her have some fun."

◆◆◆

Miguel closes the door behind the last party guest, and I wash glasses and plates with my sleeves rolled up, shoes kicked off.

He comes up behind me and puts his arms around my waist. "We survived," he says into my hair. "Let's try to remember not to do this next year."

Outside, the snow is gathering in white mounds along the edge of the house. Flakes swirl in the air, like confetti, like dust, so fast they are impossible to tell apart, to understand, to catch and keep with one's hands.

Two nights from now, Miguel will refuse to go with me to my office holiday party because his mother will need him to change a lock, bake some bread, take her away from heartbreak avenue and make her whole again.

"Can't you skip the party?" Miguel will ask. "You always say you hate those things."

"I'm already dressed."

"So?"

"So I'm going," I'll say. "The only question is whether you are."

"C'mon. Don't act like it's that big a deal."

At the party that night, Tommy Erickson will sidle up to me with a bourbon on the rocks, and he will make a joke, but I won't laugh. I'll take his glass from him and set it down, and then Tommy Erickson will follow me down the hallway, past my office and his office and everyone else's, the small spaces where we try and get things done, try and shut everything out and focus, try and try and try until we've run out of trying. At the end of the hallway is the copier room with its automated light that will switch on when we enter, shining onto the table of staplers and hole punches and boxes of every size of paper clip you could possibly want—except we won't.

Tommy Erickson will lift me onto the table, and I will let him. He'll shove the door closed. The automatic fixture will eventually turn off, kick us into darkness. We will not need the light.

FOUND & LOST

Matilde was nowhere in the apartment, not curled atop the television, not crouched below the bed. Eleanor checked every kitchen cabinet and even the broken dryer, calling Matilde's name.

The last time Eleanor had seen the white cat was last night when Matilde had scampered under the couch while Eleanor and Solomon argued about Arnie.

"Have you seen Matilde?" she asked Solomon now, standing in the bathroom doorway as he brushed his teeth.

He shook his head at her in the mirror.

He had gone to bed three hours after Eleanor. "You were the last one up," she said. He had slept on the edge of their double bed that until three months ago had been only his.

Solomon spit in the sink. "So?"

"Did you let her out by accident? Will you help me look for her?"

"I'm meeting Jared in a minute."

"For what?"

"You're not the only one who likes to go out for breakfast."

"Can't you be late?" Eleanor asked. "Jared's never on time."

Solomon pushed past her. "She'll come back. She always does."

Eleanor thought of places where Matilde might be. She hoped the cat was not cold. It was so easy to get lost here.

Even though Eleanor had lived in the city for almost two years, she rarely drove and had to take out a map to get anywhere. Arnie's conference was across town, and he had suggested a diner near his hotel that claimed to serve the city's best waffles. Eleanor made three wrong turns and finally pulled over and asked for directions.

This never would have happened if Solomon had driven. He was of the city: He knew which deli made the best Reuben, which taquería served homemade salsa, which club was just enough on the good side of seedy to be hip. He knew the store that sold roasted, salted pistachios in the back, in hot paper bags. He knew what car mechanic to trust, and where to get the best coffee, at Wide-Eyed.

"Don't drink it with sugar," Solomon said the first time, taking the two packets from Eleanor's hand.

"It's too bitter."

"Bitterness isn't bad," he said. "You've got to enjoy what things really are, not doctor them into something different."

Eleanor took a sip and then set the mug down and slid it away on the table. "I can't do this."

He pushed the mug back. "I have complete faith in you."

She took another sip, imagining what it would be like if she had no comparison. In the end, he was right. Everyone could learn to live with bitterness. It just depended on changing the notion of sweet, or forgetting it.

Last night, before the argument, Eleanor's mother had called. "When are you coming home? Your father wants to know."

"Does Dad need me to come home?"

"You know him. He doesn't ask for much."

"Mom, it's hard for me to take days off," Eleanor said. "I'm trying to save them for vacation next year."

"Where are you going?"

"I don't know yet."

"So you're not coming home?"

"I'll be home at Christmas. That's just two months. Is that okay?"

"If going on a trip with your new boyfriend makes you happy, then of course that's what we want," her mother said. "Did I tell you I saw Arnie the other day?"

The first time Eleanor saw Arnie was at the public pool, when they were both sixteen. A towel was flung over his legs, another over his shoulders, another over his head. He was reading a book. She had teased him about it endlessly.

Now, as Arnie emerged from the elevator in the hotel lobby, he opened his arms upon seeing Eleanor. He was so tall her face became buried in his sweater, which smelled, as always, of chamomile. She closed her eyes and held on.

"Hey," he said. "You okay?"

Eleanor stepped back. "You smell like home."

He laughed. "I hope that's a good thing."

Arnie had two hours before his conference started again. They chose a booth, ordered waffles with raspberries and extra butter.

"I see your parents all the time," he said. "Sometimes they stop by the office to ask a legal question."

"I'm sorry—I'll ask them to stop."

"Don't do that," he said. "It used to be hard, you know, at first, but now I like seeing them."

They talked for the next hour, and the room embraced them with light and warmth. Then he signaled for the check. "Hey," he said. "I have news. No, it's good. I wanted to tell you before your mom found out and told you first."

Eleanor squeezed her napkin with both her hands.

When Eleanor walked into the apartment, she called out for Matilde, who sauntered from the kitchen.

"I told you," Solomon said, splayed out across the couch, holding the remote, the television silenced.

"Where was she?" Eleanor rubbed her face against the cat's.

"I was thinking." Solomon sat up and motioned Eleanor to sit down, but she remained. "How about we go someplace special for Christmas."

"I'm going home. You said you had to work."

"What if I told you I talked my boss into letting me off, and I found tickets to a place you'll want to go."

"Where?"

"Vancouver. Paris. Guadalajara. One of those."

"My mom would kill me."

"You'll be far away. She won't be able to kill you."

"Solly . . ."

"You don't have to decide now. Just think about it. Please? It'll be our first real Christmas. I want us to remember it. "

Christmas seemed easier than so many other things he had asked.

"By the way," he said, "she came home because of me."

"What?"

"I canceled with Jared, and I walked around with a damn can of tuna. When that didn't work, I put the can on the front steps and sat there and waited."

"How long?"

"Until she came back."

"Solly, you didn't have to."

"It doesn't matter who gave her to you," he said. "She's ours now."

WHAT SHE WANTS

The scale blinked back two and a half more pounds than last week, and because Ginny didn't want to look or feel any heavier today—not for the hour-and-a-half trip with her parents to Charlotte, North Carolina, to take care of any last details for Mary Elizabeth's wedding in three weeks—Ginny chose a pair of black Bermuda shorts, a black polo shirt, and some black sandals. Black said that things did not exist; it was the color of forgetting, perfect for the day.

Ginny put the last of her toiletries in her overnight bag. Her parents would arrive any minute to get her, and all her mother would talk about the whole way there would be the wedding and how beautiful Mary Elizabeth was going to look—on this point, Ginny would agree—and how wonderful it would be to see Mary Elizabeth's dear, dear friends at the wedding, friends who all happened to be slim and would probably show up looking like boutique mannequins but with handsome husbands on their arms. Ginny wished again that her boyfriend, Joe, had decided to go with them to Charlotte this weekend. His excuse, that it was "a family thing," was his excuse for anything he wanted to get out of, and what was never said out loud was that he could be family if he wanted. Ginny had too much pride to suggest such a thing, to offer up her ring size and her love of emeralds versus diamonds. She had tried to bribe him to go on the trip by promising to stop at the hunting and fishing outlet just outside the city, but he had crossed his arms and shaken his head, said he had way too much work to do, and Ginny had not resorted to begging. At least Joe had offered to watch her Labrador Retriever, Marmalade, while she was gone.

From the street, there was a tap-tap of the horn, and Ginny grabbed her bag and keys. As Ginny approached her parents' gray Buick humming on the street, her mother, Rose, was already rolling down the passenger side window. "We're not going to a funeral" was the first and only thing she said.

"I know, Ma." Ginny leaned down and put her face squarely in the frame of the window. "Dad," she said, "can you pop open the trunk?"

"Need help with your bag, honey?" he asked, not snapping open his seatbelt.

"Nope." She stood up. "I got it." She'd been saying that line her entire life.

The car smelled like popcorn and menthol. Her father, Harry, always got a free bag of popcorn at the hardware store, but the popcorn often fell from his hands and into the space between his seat and door, and you could find it mashed into the Buick's carpet even when he had not gone to the hardware store in weeks. The menthol smell was from the cream that her mother used on her hands, cream she claimed helped her arthritis but gave her a headache, yet it was a sacrifice she must endure. Ginny tried to breathe out of her mouth.

Mary Elizabeth called while they were on the road and said there was a problem with the alterations of her bridal gown and maybe she should find a different dress. Her fiancé, Lionel, had picked out the strapless, empire-waistline dress as well as told Mary Elizabeth which seamstress to use for the fitting. Ginny could not determine if her sister had ever liked the dress, and it was pointless to ask if she did. Mary Elizabeth's response would likely be a shrug, as was often the case. By the time they reached Charlotte—an hour and a half of driving and twenty minutes at a rest stop later—her mother had complained of a headache, nausea, and stomach cramps, all of which, she insisted, had been brought on by her worry for Mary Elizabeth.

As they sped up Park Road in the Buick, Rose pointed to a bakery. "Over there, Harry. Pull in."

"We've got to get to Mary Elizabeth. It's quarter after eleven." He pointed a thick finger at the clock in the car as if he needed confirmation. "We said we'd be there by now."

"Mary Elizabeth might be upset," Rose said. "We should get her a glazed donut."

"Ma." Ginny leaned forward from the back seat, and the seatbelt cut into her chest and stomach like a bad pageant ribbon. "She's trying not to eat so much sugar these days, remember?"

"If you two are going to gang up on me, fine. We'll skip it. But if Mary Elizabeth's hungry, don't blame me."

"There's a place that serves sushi down the road from her condo. We can go there later." Ginny leaned back again. "Dad, could you turn up the AC?"

"Sushi? You mean raw fish?" Rose asked.

"She likes it."

"She shouldn't be eating things like that."

"Let's just see what she wants when we get there," said Ginny, who, like her mother, had a headache, but Ginny didn't say a word about the scent of heavy perfume that her mother had dabbed on at the rest stop, a scent which had now become inextricably mixed with the smell of menthol and popcorn. "Dad, could you turn up the AC just a little more?"

Harry pointed as they passed a street. "Is this the turn?"

"Yep, that was it," Ginny said, not glancing back.

"Harry, why didn't you turn?"

"Just go one more block, Dad, and then make a right."

"If you knew that was the street, why didn't you turn?" Rose said.

"I didn't know. That's why I asked."

"Well you can't ask and then just pass it by."

"It's okay, Ma. I know the way."

"We're going to be late." Rose crossed her arms. "We told Mary Elizabeth we'd be there by 11:15."

"It's okay," Ginny said. "We'll get there when we get there."

Mary Elizabeth's hair was caramel brown and as soft as a cat's, unlike Ginny's, which was brownish red and thick and more like the coat of a terrier. Mary Elizabeth was slender and tall, clear-skinned and high-cheekboned, unlike Ginny, or Rose, as a matter of fact, who were both round-faced, their bodies broad and substantial, words Harry liked to use when attempting to compliment them. Ginny reminded herself that for all her physical failings—her inability to sprint, her tendency to trip, her bad aim (she'd always been the last one chosen for teams in gym class)—she was luckier than Mary Elizabeth in the ways of life. It was Ginny, not Mary Elizabeth, who had a yellow Labrador Retriever, a three-bedroom bungalow with a back porch, and no credit card debt. It was Ginny, not Mary Elizabeth, who had a fabulous boss who let her sneak out of work for hair appointments, and it was Ginny, not Mary Elizabeth, who would likely bear children, mostly because Ginny had always wanted them and Mary Elizabeth acted as if they didn't exist, especially when confronted with a woman pushing a stroller.

In school, Ginny had excelled in all subjects, but especially in science and math, while Mary Elizabeth had struggled with equations and logic and spelling and sentence structure—basically anything requiring sequence and order. Mary Elizabeth had a flair for painting and drawing, and she had doodled her way through junior high and high school, the margins of all her notebooks jammed with squiggly lines and circles. Back then, Ginny had thought that Mary Elizabeth was doomed never to get in to college because her grades were so poor, but as luck would have it, or rather as Mary Elizabeth's luck would have it, she landed a scholarship to a school of art and design, and Harry had been extremely relieved. Ginny only knew this because he cried at Mary Elizabeth's graduation, as if the simple act of her having finally finished something was monumental.

Ginny was an accountant while Mary Elizabeth was a graphic designer who barely eked out a living. Of course, Lionel would change all that. He was a Jr. or a III—Ginny couldn't remember which, in part because the family had only met him once, months ago, for a dinner when they had been visiting Mary Elizabeth in Charlotte. He'd taken them out, of course, ordered wine and appetizers along with the entrées, and then asked for a tray of desserts so they could try everything. It was enough to make her mother swoon. Lionel worked but didn't have to; Mary Elizabeth wouldn't have to, either. That was lucky, Ginny knew, but she reminded herself she loved her work and was grateful to have purpose and meaning in her every day, and what sort of meaning and purpose was there in waking up each morning with nothing to do?

Ginny had been lucky in other ways too: she had never had a steady boyfriend until college while Mary Elizabeth had had a new boyfriend every other month throughout high school. Who would want an entourage of men? It seemed exhausting, all that effort, attracting men, attempting to keep them happy, and then being okay once they broke it off, if you didn't get to it first. For three years now—most of which, until recently, Mary Elizabeth had spent entering and exiting relationships—Ginny had had Joe. He was steady and loyal, the kind of man who could be counted on to drop you off and pick you up at the airport at the exact time you had requested, the kind of man who checked the air pressure on your tires before you left on a trip, and the kind of man who offered to be the designated driver if everyone else wanted to drink. Though he was only thirty-nine and had only recently become assistant principal at the academy where he had taught English for over a decade, he had a substantial IRA, had paid off eight years of a fifteen-year mortgage on a two-bedroom house, owned a cat named Machu Picchu (not because he'd been there but because he liked the sound of it), and took a multivitamin every morning without fail. Who could be luckier than Ginny with a man like that?

Mary Elizabeth wasn't waiting at the door for them when they arrived at her condo. Ginny had to knock several times and buzz the doorbell over and over before Mary Elizabeth answered, a phone pressed to her ear.

"Sorry," she mouthed and then covered the receiver. "It's the caterer," she whispered, pointing at the phone. "Yes, I understand. Of course. Uh-huh, uh-huh," she said into the phone and rolled her eyes and mouthed, "Oh. My. God."

After hanging up, Mary Elizabeth gave a quick hug to her parents, and then to Ginny she said, "I don't know what the deal is, but they're wanting to change the menu. Maybe we just shouldn't go with them."

"How many things do they want to change?" Ginny asked.

"I don't know. The shrimp, the mini quiches, and some other things. This just doesn't feel like the right company to work with anymore."

"It'd be hard to find a new caterer at this late a date," Ginny said. "Do you want me to call them?"

"No, no. I'll figure it out."

"It's going to be a perfect wedding," Rose said, reaching out and clasping Mary Elizabeth's hands.

Mary Elizabeth wriggled her hands free. "No wedding is perfect, Mom."

"Yours will be. I promise."

"Well, it won't be perfect if we don't have food, and I have no dress yet because the seamstress is running way behind."

"You'll have food," Ginny said.

"Your sister will call the caterer and the seamstress," Rose said.

"I don't want Ginny to call."

"Ma, she's fine. She'll figure it out."

"I'm trying to help," Rose said to Ginny. "Why aren't you trying to help your baby sister?"

"Let's go get something to eat," Ginny said. "Will that help?"

Mary Elizabeth shrugged, so Ginny herded her family out the door.

Eating was what the family did when they ran out of useful words. When they had arguments that were going nowhere, which often happened when they argued, they used their forks and knives to scratch their discontent across the plates. They scowled at the bread but ate it. They pouted but added butter to it. When they ate at home, Harry sat at the table but turned on the TV, which was always within eyesight and earshot, and during tense times, especially if Rose was upset, he flicked on the news, preferring the sound of someone assuring him there was something worse in the world than whatever shrouded his house.

Rose never apologized, even when it was obvious she was wrong, even when the evidence stenched up the room and her daughters pointed it out. What Rose did do was bake sugar cookies and boil hot chocolate. Ginny ate and drank these tokens of contrition while Mary Elizabeth had spent her whole life refusing them, pushing the steaming cups away, shoving warm plates across tables.

"Darling," Rose said, putting her hand over Mary Elizabeth's as soon as they sat down at the restaurant. "You have to eat."

The place was popular, and they'd had to wait twenty minutes for a table.

"I'm not hungry."

"Why are we here if you're not going to eat?"

"We need to eat, too, Ma," Ginny said. "None of us have had lunch."

"How can I eat when my child won't eat?"

"*I'm* eating," Ginny said.

"Please, order something. Eat," Mary Elizabeth said. "I'm fine."

"She said to eat." Harry opened the menu. "Look, Rose, they have your favorite dish."

"I'm not eating if she isn't."

"Mary Elizabeth will eat." Ginny gave her sister the look. "You'll order something, right?"

"Sure." Mary Elizabeth brushed her fingers across the shiny menu but did not open it.

"They have chicken picatta?" Rose asked.

"They have lemon swordfish." Harry pointed to the menu.

"Since when do I like that?"

"You got that citrus chicken salad last week at K&W."

"How is that lemon swordfish?"

"It's got citrus," Harry said. "You liked it, right?"

"I want chicken picatta."

"Ma, this isn't an Italian restaurant," Ginny said. "They have seafood. Just get the lemon swordfish."

"Is it any good?"

Mary Elizabeth shrugged. "I've never gotten it."

"I'm not getting anything," Rose said.

"C'mon, Ma." Ginny glared at her sister, who was staring out the window. "Mary Elizabeth, why don't you tell us what *is* good, then."

"I always get sushi."

"I'm gonna see if they'll make me chicken picatta," Rose said and snapped the menu closed.

Ginny was still 31 pounds over her target weight of 126. In the back of her bedroom closet—so far back that Ginny had to strain to reach it, which she only did when she was having a terrible day—Ginny's past hung: jeans with elastic waistbands, shirts with gathers, bulky sweaters that dropped far below her waist. These garments were the only physical evidence of that era of her life, from ages sixteen to twenty-seven. After that, she'd lost 50 pounds and kept it (mostly) off. But now that she was thirty-four, she wanted to take off the rest. Though she would never admit it, Ginny had this idea that if she slimmed to 126, even if it was hard, everything else would come easier.

To lose weight, you had to count more than calories. You had to count—and manage—your liabilities, your tendencies, your weaknesses. In Ginny's mind, there were four kinds of weight. There was the first and best: necessary weight—the kind that kept you alive and consisted of muscle and bone and organs and nerves. There was fatty weight, the kind that you needed just enough of to keep you from drowning in saltwater and to help you bear children. There was extra weight—the good stuff but in abundant supply, the kind of weight that you needed only in a hostage situation, that allowed you to survive for weeks but that in normal day-to-day life was excessive. Putting on this kind of weight was akin to having a tendency to buy more of something you liked just in case you couldn't find it later when you really needed it, which you rarely did. Then there was the dead weight, the total extra burden of pounds you carried of insecurities, doubts, pessimism, the kind that could not be lost by counting calories or skipping desserts, the kind that made up who you were at your core, that drove you to get good grades and good jobs but that allowed you to talk yourself out of thinking you deserved anything better than whatever came your way when it came to people, relationships, love. Dead as in the kind that has the potential to pull you under, to let you drown.

Mary Elizabeth and Ginny excused themselves to the restroom after they'd ordered. It was a one-toilet bathroom, no stall, and Ginny bolted the lock while Mary Elizabeth hoisted herself onto the sink counter to wait. Ginny used the lone toilet while Mary Elizabeth rummaged through Ginny's purse. "Why'd you have to bring them?" Mary Elizabeth asked.

"Because they're our parents."

"You could have come separately and let them come later. Then we could be doing manis and pedis and having girl time."

"Ma would love girl time."

"I don't know how you do it, living in the same town." Mary Elizabeth fished a lipstick from Ginny's purse, pulled the gold cap off of it, and ran the color across her lips. "How's Assistant Principal Joe?"

Ginny flushed the toilet. "He's great."

Mary Elizabeth put the cap on the lipstick and tossed it back into Ginny's purse. "Why didn't he come? Still avoiding?"

"He's not avoiding anything."

"Whatever."

Ginny turned the cold and hot faucets on to wash her hands. "What's gotten into you today?"

"Nothing."

"You nervous?"

"Not really," Mary Elizabeth said. "I don't know."

"For a blushing bride, you don't seem very blushing."

"Brides don't blush." Mary Elizabeth hopped off the counter as Ginny dried her hands. "They grit their teeth and pray it'll soon be over. And anyway, happiness is relative. Not everyone is like you, Ginny, able to be at peace and accept what life brings."

"Who says I'm like that? I want things. And you—you're about to marry a man who is handsome, rich, and adores you. What else do you want?"

"Can I have that lipstick?"

Ginny dug it out of her purse and applied it to her lips, pressed them together and studied herself for a moment in the mirror. "It does look better on you."

"How much did Mom talk about the wedding on the drive?"

"Let's see. She did pause to take a breath every once in a while. And to complain about Dad's driving."

Mary Elizabeth crossed her arms. "I figured."

"Don't look so disappointed. You're making her happy, which is more than I seem to ever do." Ginny handed her the lipstick. "Here, it's yours."

Mary Elizabeth turned it over in her palm. "Don't you ever just want to run away from everything? Just escape?"

"Why would I want to do that?"

"No reason. And hey, thanks for this," Mary Elizabeth said, slipping the lipstick into her jeans pocket. "You'll always be happier than I can ever hope to be." She tucked Ginny's hair behind one ear and then the other. "And rightly so. You deserve to be happy because you are a far better person than I am."

"You're crazy," Ginny said.

"And you've got a great life, except for the Joe avoiding part."

"He's not avoiding."

"We're all avoiding. You and I and Joe and the whole world." Mary Elizabeth unbolted the bathroom door. "It's just a matter of what we're avoiding and when it will appear on our doorstep and blow up in our face."

Ginny stepped outside of the restaurant to call Joe. He didn't like being disturbed when he was working, but she wanted to know how his day was going. Maybe he was wishing that he'd come with her after all.

"Hey," he answered.

"Hi," Ginny said. "How's work going? Getting a lot done?"

"Sure. What's going on?"

"Nothing. I was just checking in."

"Has your mother stopped complaining yet?"

"Of course not." Ginny heard Marmalade bark through the phone, and then she heard a bark she didn't recognize. "Where are you?"

"Dog park," Joe said.

"Now? It's only 12:30."

"It opens at 7 a.m."

"You said you had a ton of work to do." The sun bore down on Ginny and her black outfit.

"I got it done." Joe whistled. "C'mere, boy! Marmalade, come here! Good boy."

"You're supposed to be working all day."

"Are you mad at me?" Joe asked. "I'm taking Marmalade out for exercise. I thought you'd be happy."

"I am." Ginny was sweating all over. She opened the door to the restaurant and stepped into the lobby. "I'm just—I didn't understand your day, that's all." She was going to need a paper towel bath in the restroom now.

"Everything's good here," Joe said.

"Yeah, okay," she said. "Well, have fun." She hung up and threw her phone into her purse and marched straight into the ladies' room, locking the door behind her, turning on the cold faucet and splashing water on her face even after she had cooled down.

After lunch and some errands, the family pulled the Buick into the parking lot of Mary Elizabeth's condo complex. A man was sitting on her front stoop. He had on a rumpled shirt, jean shorts, and brown Dansko clogs (Ginny didn't know men even wore those), and he was running his hands through his disheveled hair. He looked to be in his forties.

"Is that a beggar?" Rose asked.

"Sort of," Mary Elizabeth said as the man saw the car, squinted toward them, and stood up. "That's my boss."

"Farrow? What's he doing here?" Ginny asked. "Don't you have the day off?"

"I do, but . . ." Mary Elizabeth was already opening the car door, before Harry had even shut off the engine. "Can you guys just wait here for a sec?"

The three of them watched as Mary Elizabeth stalked over to Farrow. They appeared to argue, but he seemed to say only a word or two, mostly kept his mouth shut, his hands shoved in his pockets as Mary Elizabeth lit into him, gesticulating with zest. He shook his head and frowned, and Mary Elizabeth talked and talked, pointing to the car intermittently but not taking her eyes off him. She jabbed his chest with her finger.

"Do you think they're having a fight?" Rose asked.

"I'd say so," Ginny said.

"Harry, do something."

"Like what?"

"She's okay," Ginny said. "She's got the upper hand."

"How do you know?" Rose asked.

"She always does."

"That's my girl," Rose said. "I just don't want her to lose her job. That might look bad to Lionel."

Now Farrow was nodding somberly, and they walked together to the Buick, Mary Elizabeth in the lead. She tapped on the window, which Harry rolled down. "Hiya," he said.

Mary Elizabeth gestured toward her boss. "This is Farrow."

Rose leaned over to Harry's side so she could see them out Harry's window. "She's a hard worker, isn't she?"

Farrow leaned down. "Your daughter is the best. I couldn't live without her."

Ginny raised her eyebrows at Mary Elizabeth, who announced, "Farrow's leaving now. He forgot it was Saturday, my day off."

"Yes," he said, straightening up. "I was coming by to talk about an assignment. Which I shouldn't have done. Not on her day off. I thought it couldn't wait, but it can. It will. I respect her and her time off. Very much." He cleared his throat. "We'll talk later, right?" He was looking at Mary Elizabeth now.

"Like I said, he's leaving."

Rose leaned over again and said, "Mary Elizabeth is always talking about how wonderful her job is." Which was not true—Mary Elizabeth complained all the time—but Ginny resisted the urge to roll her eyes.

"Bye, Farrow," Mary Elizabeth said.

"Nice to meet you all," he said. "Really nice. I hope we meet again soon. I would really like that."

"Bye, Farrow," Mary Elizabeth repeated.

And with that, he disappeared.

Mary Elizabeth's condominium was painted a pale blue. Everywhere. Apparently Lionel Jr. or III or IV liked blue. "He says it calms him," Mary Elizabeth said to Rose and Ginny as they stood in the living room surveying the condo while Rose wondered out loud how much the condo might sell for. Harry slouched on the sofa with the TV remote in his hand, flipping channels.

"But Lionel doesn't live here," Ginny said. "You do."

"He paid for it to be painted, so I let him choose the color. Seemed fair."

"I think the color is beautiful, like a brilliant sky," Rose said.

"I feel like I'm in an aquarium," Ginny said. "I mean, not a bad aquarium. Just a very blue one."

Mary Elizabeth looked around, as if she were just now noticing the color of the walls. "I guess you're right."

"Don't listen to her," Rose said. "It's stunning. He has wonderful taste."

"No, Ginny's right. It's awful."

"I didn't say it was awful."

"It's lovely, dear."

After her mother went to lie down and her father had settled further into the couch with a baseball game on, Ginny steered Mary Elizabeth into the kitchen.

"What was that about?" Ginny asked.

"What was what about?" Mary Elizabeth opened the fridge and stared into the cold.

"Um, your weirdo boss showing up at your house?"

"He's not weird."

"You used to call him General Unibrow."

"That was two years ago," Mary Elizabeth said. She reached for a big tub of yogurt and snapped open the lid.

"Is he bothering you?"

"No." Mary Elizabeth rummaged in her silverware drawer for a spoon.

"Does he show up here a lot?"

"Not really." Mary Elizabeth ate exactly two spoonfuls of yogurt before closing the yogurt tub and returning it to the fridge.

"Mary Elizabeth, look at me. What's going on?"

Mary Elizabeth let out an enormous sigh. "Just don't be like Mom, okay?"

"Of course I won't. I'm not like her."

"I sorta did a bad thing. I mean, not on purpose or anything," Mary Elizabeth said.

"What kind of bad thing?"

"It didn't seem bad at the time."

"Mary Elizabeth, what did you do?"

"I kinda let something happen with Farrow."

"This Farrow? Farrow Farrow?"

Mary Elizabeth was glowering now. "No, the other one."

"But doesn't he have the maniacal ex-wife who calls up the office drunk and cusses out whatever employee answers the phone?"

"You're sounding like Mom. You know that, right? All judgy?"

"Sorry. I just meant—never mind. Go on."

"Yes, his ex-wife is crazy, but that's why he divorced her."

"You also told me you hated him," Ginny said.

"When did I say that?"

"I don't know. Six months, a year ago? More than once."

"Oh. Well, that's the thing. I did, or at least I thought I did. But maybe I don't."

"Start from the beginning. Did you sleep with him?"

"How is that the beginning? But no," Mary Elizabeth said. "Of course not."

"Thank God."

"But."

"But what?"

Mary Elizabeth plopped into a chair at the kitchen table and started sliding the salt and pepper shakers back and forth between her hands. Sometimes the shakers knocked into one another with a clack. "We had this happy hour for work a while back," Mary Elizabeth said, not meeting Ginny's stare, "and we all had a bit too much to drink, and he and I were the last ones out, and I was gonna call a cab, but Farrow offered to give me a lift and . . ."

"And what?"

"Well, so on the ride here we talked about proximity and white space, and then we talked about Milton Glaser and his not-as-famous DC Comics work, and we both love DC Comics—I didn't even know Farrow liked comics—"

"You like comics?"

Mary Elizabeth stopped fiddling with the shakers and blinked up at Ginny. "Of course I do." She resumed the fiddling, the sliding, the clacking. "Anyway, Farrow and I were talking about the rise of graphic novels, and by that time we had had another drink or two here—"

"Wait, what?"

"Well, maybe I asked him in. He was interesting. I didn't know he was that interesting, and I didn't want to stop talking, but then . . . I don't mean to say 'but then' like it's bad because it didn't mean anything at all."

"What didn't mean anything at all?"

"Maybe he kissed me. Or I kissed him." Mary Elizabeth covered her face with her hands. "Or both."

"Once? More than once?" And when her sister wouldn't answer, Ginny asked, "More than kissed?"

Mary Elizabeth uncovered her face. "Don't look at me like that. We've hung out a few times since then. That's all. He's really interesting. And nothing has happened since then. I mean, not exactly."

"Mary Elizabeth, what are you doing?"

"I don't know." She let out another enormous sigh, and tears rimmed her eyes. It reminded Ginny of the time Ginny had made Mary Elizabeth confess she had smoked marijuana with her friends in her bedroom. Ginny could smell it all throughout the house, but she acted as if she didn't know what it was and kept asking questions until Mary Elizabeth broke down and told her. Mary Elizabeth had been fourteen, and their parents had been out of town and had left Ginny in charge. Mary Elizabeth had cried so hard after her confession, begging Ginny not to tell, that even though Ginny had been furious with Mary Elizabeth, she knew, looking at her sister's face swept with tears, she would not tell on her. Even if she had, her mother would have blamed Ginny for letting the whole episode happen under her watch.

"He told me three days ago he loves me," Mary Elizabeth said. "And he doesn't want me to get married. What do I do?"

"Quit your job. Now," Ginny said.

Mary Elizabeth blinked at her.

"Are you telling me you think you love him, too?" Ginny asked.

"I'm confused." Mary Elizabeth was blinking rapidly now. "I'm getting married in three weeks."

"I know."

"But, but," Mary Elizabeth said, "would it be horrible if I didn't?"

Ginny opened a kitchen cabinet and retrieved a glass and filled it with water. She set it down in front of Mary Elizabeth and then pulled a chair back and sat down, too. "Okay," she said. "Let's talk this through. Don't worry. We'll figure it out."

Rose was still napping and Harry was still sucked into the couch watching a game when Ginny walked Mary Elizabeth out to her car. The humidity felt thick, like butter.

"You sure this is what you want?" Ginny asked.

Mary Elizabeth nodded somberly and clicked open the door with her key fob.

"Do you want me to go with you? It'll just take me a second to grab my purse." A mosquito landed on Ginny's arm, and she squashed it.

"The worst part won't be telling him." Mary Elizabeth got into the car and rolled down the window. "It'll be telling Mom."

"I'll be here," Ginny offered. They were words she had offered to everyone her whole life.

"How do I look?" Mary Elizabeth asked. She adjusted the rearview mirror toward her and pressed her lips together.

"How are you supposed to look?"

"Like I'm not making the biggest mistake of all my mistakes like everyone will think I am," she said. "Like I know what the hell I'm doing." Mary Elizabeth pressed the start button, and the engine turned over. "But mostly, I'm supposed to look beautiful, no matter what. Isn't that the rule?"

"Hurry back," Ginny said. "We'll be waiting."

When Ginny had weighed more, people had not noticed much about her. When she'd been heavier, people had looked past her, rarely commenting on her clothes or the way she had styled her hair, or her jewelry. It always seemed illogical: that extra weight made her less visible instead of more. When Ginny had lost the fifty pounds, people started commenting on her eye color, any new blouse or cute shoes, or even a scarf she had worn a hundred times that no one had bothered to observe before, as if Ginny had suddenly become apparent.

It had never occurred to her to wonder what Mary Elizabeth might feel like being noticed all the time. Ginny had assumed it was something she wanted, but now she had to consider what it might be like to have people see every inch of you, even the inches you wanted no one to see.

Two and a half hours later, Ginny was handing a bowl of popcorn to her father, still nestled in the couch, when Mary Elizabeth walked in the door. "Hey guys." She set her white pocketbook on the table by the door. She rattled the keys, still in her hand.

"There you are," Rose said, getting up from an easy chair where she had been flipping through the RSVPs, sorting and organizing them, as best as Ginny could determine, by the people she liked and the people she didn't and those about whom she had yet to form an opinion. Rose said, "Ginny wouldn't let me call you."

"I said you could call her from my phone."

"You know I don't know how to use those things. They're too complicated with their screens and words. I just want numbers and buttons."

"Do you have any seltzer water?" Harry asked Mary Elizabeth. "This popcorn's going to make me thirsty."

"How did it go?" Ginny asked.

"How did what go?" Rose asked. "Ginny said you had some important errand, but she wouldn't tell me what it was. Where were you?" She clapped. "Did you see Lionel? Did he surprise you with a gift? What did he give you?"

"Nothing, I mean yes, I saw Lionel, but . . ." Mary Elizabeth tossed her keys on the table. "The wedding's off."

"What?" Rose reached for the back of a chair and held on. "What happened?"

Mary Elizabeth glanced at Ginny.

"What is it?" Rose asked. She turned to Ginny. "What did you do?"

"I didn't do anything," Ginny said.

Rose turned to Mary Elizabeth. "Did your sister make you do this?"

"Of course I didn't," Ginny said. "I had nothing to do with it."

"I don't want to marry him."

"Did you catch him with someone else?" Rose asked.

"No, it's not like that. I'm just not . . . he's not my person."

"What are you talking about?" Rose stumbled to the coffee table and grabbed a magazine and started fanning her face. She was blocking Harry's view.

Harry looked up from the TV. "Is everything okay?"

"The wedding's been called off," Ginny said.

He sat up and frowned toward Mary Elizabeth. "You called it off or he did?"

"I did."

"Oh, okay." His face relaxed again. He settled back against the couch, shifting his position one cushion over so he could see the TV, and resumed watching the game.

"They were going to get married," Rose said to him through tears. "Aren't you going to do something?"

"She said it was her choice."

"I'm fine, Dad, really."

"Good, honey. Just let me know if you need something."

Rose's sniffles grew louder.

"Rosie, don't do that," Harry said. "It's gonna be alright. Sit down with me. Come here." He patted the cushion beside him.

"That's all you have to say?"

"Ma, this isn't Dad's fault," Ginny said.

"What about you? You're not going to do anything either?"

"Mom, there's nothing to do," Mary Elizabeth said.

"Well if no one's going to do anything," Rose said, "I'm going to the car." She stormed down the hall and into the guest room and emerged a moment later with her big block of a purse and strode to the door. "I want to go home." She slammed the front door behind her.

The game chirped on, the announcer's voice murmuring as a timeout ended and playing continued.

"Don't worry." Harry stood. "I'll talk to your mother." He stepped toward the door but then stopped, eyes still fixed on the game. A batter was at the plate, strike one, strike two.

"Dad," Ginny said.

"Hang on, hang on. The inning's almost over. Just two seconds." He shouted at the TV, "C'mon!"

The sisters exchanged glances. "Why don't you go talk to her?" Ginny asked.

Mary Elizabeth shook her head. "I'll just make her more unhappy."

Ginny's stomach churned. "Okay," Ginny said. *Fine, fine, fine.*

The Buick was parked in the shade, but the day had gotten even warmer and muggier. How was that possible? Her mother was in the passenger seat already, arms wrapped around the purse in her lap, but the engine was not on. Ginny opened the driver's side door and got in. "You can't stay out here all day. It's hot. Don't you want to come back inside?"

"Tell your father I want to go home."

"I think it'd be better if we stayed and talked."

"About what?" Rose sniffled.

"Ma, it's what Mary Elizabeth wants."

Her mother turned away and to the passenger window. "Sometimes I don't know if you girls know what you're doing. You think you know what you want, but maybe you want the wrong thing."

Ginny put her hands on the steering wheel and moved it from side to side until it clicked in place and locked. "I think we know what we're doing." The car was getting hotter, and Ginny rolled down the driver's side window. She reached across her mother's lap and rolled down the passenger window, too. "She doesn't want to marry him. Do you want her to be unhappy?" It was useless to ask her mother this. There was no reasoning with her.

"I don't want her to end up like you."

Ginny's chest tightened. "You mean unmarried?"

"No," Rose said. "That's not what I mean, though you'll accuse me of that, I'm sure." She unlatched her purse, found a handkerchief and dabbed at her forehead and temples. She folded the handkerchief and tucked it back in and gripped her purse handles.

"I won't accuse you of anything," Ginny said.

"Do you know how many times your father had to ask me to marry him before I said yes?"

"Yes, Ma. Four times. I know the story."

"But do you know why I didn't say yes until the fourth time?"

"Because you wanted to torture him?" Ginny immediately regretted saying it, but her mother did not seem to have heard it anyway.

Rose continued, "Because I wanted to make sure he meant it. The first time a man asks you to marry him, he's got his nerve on the line. The second time he asks, his power is on the line: he wants to see if he can change your mind. The third time, it's his pride on the line: you say no, it might mean he really isn't worthy. The fourth time, all he has left is his heart on the line."

"Why are you telling me this? Lionel didn't ask Mary Elizabeth four times."

"But he would have. And anyway I'm not talking about Mary Elizabeth."

"Then what are you talking about?"

"You're ready to say yes, and Joe hasn't even asked you once."

Ginny's whole body tensed, and she shut her eyes. There were so many arguments caught in her throat: Joe loved her, he was just taking his time, and just because he hadn't asked didn't mean . . .

Ginny swallowed all of it. She opened her eyes and stared out the windshield. She was sweating all over. Beads of it fell down her neck and into the fabric of her shirt, nowhere to escape. "You don't get to decide who we pick, who we love, or what we do," Ginny said.

"I'm your mother."

"I don't care. You don't get a say anymore."

Rose unlatched her purse again, yanked the handkerchief out, and then dabbed her eyes and put it back. "You don't know what it's like to be a mother."

"You're right, I don't and I might never know because apparently I'm making all the wrong decisions."

Across the complex parking lot, a woman was dragging two children by the hands toward a minivan with a bent fender and faded paint. The woman had a bag on one shoulder overflowing with beach towels, and hanging from her other arm was a life jacket and an inner tube. One of the kids was screaming and trying to sit down on the asphalt, but the mother kept tugging the child up and toward the vehicle. Finally, she hustled them both into the back, strapped them in their car seats and started the van.

Rose coughed and opened her purse but didn't touch the handkerchief. She shut the purse again and faced forward, looking through the windshield at nothing. The clasp on her string of pearls had come unhooked. The two ends were connected but barely hanging on to each other. Ginny reached behind her mother's neck and fastened them tightly together. She opened the driver's door and stepped out of the car. She closed the door and leaned down to look in the open window at her mother, just as she had that morning. "We're not leaving today, Ma. Mary Elizabeth needs us, so you can sit out here for as long as you want or you can come back inside. I'm going to fix us some dinner."

Ginny was almost to the condo door when her mother called out, "What are you making?" Her mother pulled on her door handle. "Maybe we should make one of your sister's old favorites."

"I'm making what I want to make," Ginny said. Tacos filled with chicken thighs that had been sprinkled with cumin, smoked paprika, and chili powder and sautéed in olive oil. Tacos that were topped with chopped onion, cilantro, jalapeños, lime juice, and a dollop of sour cream. God she was starving. She would have to run to Harris Teeter for some things, but that was okay. She would make guacamole, too, and eat it with those Xóchitl chips she loved, if she could find them at the store, and she would call Joe after dinner, and she would apologize for being grouchy, but she would also tell him they needed to talk when she got home, and no matter what happened in that conversation, no matter how much or how little was said, she would ask him for what she wanted, and if he couldn't give it to her, or if he didn't want to, then that was an outcome she would accept, not hope for but accept, and regardless Ginny would move forward, yes, she would do that, with or without him. Now she just wanted to make her favorite food for herself and for her family.

Back inside the condo, Mary Elizabeth was slouched next to Harry, her feet on the coffee table, her head resting against the back of the couch, but she sat up as Ginny walked in. A Chili's commercial belted out a jingle about baby back ribs.

A few paces behind Ginny, Rose followed, and Mary Elizabeth sprang up and went to her mother and put her arms around her. "I'm sorry, Mom," she said. "I really am."

"Everything okay?" Harry asked. "Y'all missed the best part of the game."

Rose rubbed Mary Elizabeth's back with her one free hand—the other still held the big box of a purse—and said, "I just want you to be happy."

"I know you liked Lionel."

Then Rose put her other hand, even with the purse, on Mary Elizabeth's back, too, and held on. "The truth is I wasn't sure he was good enough for you."

Ginny shook her head but smiled, and Mary Elizabeth mouthed "thank you" to Ginny before letting her mother go.

PASSENGER

The inn's walls were as thin as tea leaves, but not the kind that foretold peace and good fortune. Marta and Leopold Everhart were arguing in the next room, and Leticia could hear all of it. The arguing had begun as soon as the morning sun had dissipated the night's darkness.

Leopold wanted to take a side trip that Marta insisted was ridiculous.

"Don't you think I matter, too?" he said. Leticia had never heard Leopold raise his voice before.

"Oh, of course you do," Marta said. "Stop being so dramatic."

"I'm trying to get you to listen."

"I've been listening for twenty-two years. No one wants to go on your silly trip. Go alone."

"This is supposed to be *our* trip," Leopold said.

"It's only *our* trip if you stop with this selfishness."

"Maybe the Smiths want to go."

"Fine," Marta said. "You ask them. See what they say."

Leticia no longer liked being referred to in this way, as a unit with Ted, not as two individuals, although being a part of a couple was all she had wanted when she was younger, especially watching as the girls with whom she had gone to college had one by one received a diamond ring.

From the Everharts' room, Leopold made a muffled remark, and Marta punctured the walls with a laugh. Its cadence—a sharp rising and falling—was like the bell that had rung at the end of Leticia's every school day in Mexico, marking freedom from the confines of *preparatoria* and its confessions and Catholic uniforms.

An hour later, while the two couples ate breakfast together at the inn's restaurant in California Valley, Marta chattered on at a mighty clip. She had large teeth, a round face, and a thick row of bangs. She kept her hair dyed black to cover the gray that had crept in years ago. Marta was a decade older than Leticia, and she always admonished Leticia like a child—for speaking too softly and for wearing clothes that did not flatter her figure: "What are you hiding, Leti?" Marta did everything with a splash: wore bright colors, donned chunky beaded necklaces and bracelets, talked the most and the loudest, chose blouses with low necklines and big shoulder pads, and insisted on putting on those miniskirts that all the American women—even the ones Leticia thought should not—were wearing now. Marta believed in embracing her body and self. She reminded Leticia of the girls who had lived in Leticia's college dormitory, girls who had said hello to Leticia but never invited her into their rooms, never sat with her in the cafeteria, girls who'd worn curlers out in the hallway, where people could see them, or who had kissed men in broad daylight. They had no shame. Shame was like a wet dress: it threatened to show even the secret parts of someone, and this threat kept Leticia from daring.

As Marta talked on at breakfast, Leopold stirred sunny-side up eggs around on his plate, the yolks becoming a yellow river on a white plain. His hands shook just a little, the way Ted's did after a particularly bad night of drinking, when it was only one or two in the afternoon, before Ted's beloved three o'clock hour.

Leopold set down his fork and wiped his mouth with the napkin. "Who wants to hike today in Sugarloaf Ridge?"

Marta smeared some more strawberry jam onto her toast, smoothing it out with her knife, and Ted reached for the clear pitcher full of orange juice, poured himself some, and chugged it down while scanning the restaurant, perhaps searching for signs of a bar. Ted probably hadn't heard Leopold at all. Sometimes Ted was better off drunk, really—at least then people expected less of him. Leticia pitied Leopold in this moment, ignored by his best friend, and despite the fact that she had no interest in hiking, she drew in a deep breath.

"See?" Marta arched her eyebrows. "No one wants to go on your trip."

"I do." Leticia's voice squeaked, which it did when she was not sure of something, when she wanted to remain small.

"To Sugarloaf? Hiking? Are you making a joke?" Marta had a way of tumbling down everyone's decisions. Once, many years ago, when Leticia had confided to Marta that she planned to one day give piano lessons to *el nene*, Marta had told her, "Do you really think that he is going to want to learn music over a sport? He's a boy, Leticia. Boys need to move."

"I want to go," Leticia said now, right to Marta's face. She folded her napkin and tucked it under the white china plate on which her Danish sat, the apricot jelly glistening up at her.

Leopold was beaming. "Well, that's terrific."

Marta gave a little huff. "Have it your way," she said. "See what you think of it when the day comes to an end. It's too hot to be outside all day exhausting yourselves, but you go on. I'll manage Ted somehow."

"Me? What?" Ted said.

Marta patted him on the hand. "Nothing, darling. Your wife just made a bad decision. Nothing an afternoon drink won't fix for you."

On weekends, Ted always drank his first cocktail at three o'clock— anything before that hour was out of the question, but after somehow seemed, if not sophisticated, then at least respectable to him. Long ago, Leticia had given up trying to keep Ted in line and manage his alcohol intake, given up begging him to have slightly less, especially at parties, where they often stayed entirely too late. She should have been the designated driver in the marriage, yet with Ted's inability to stop himself, coupled with Leticia's inability to move past her fear of steering any kind of powerful engine, they were often stuck at places longer than either one of them liked. It was at those times that Leticia regretted most that she had never learned to drive.

He didn't have to quit drinking completely, just slow it down, cut some of it out. And Ted would try. At least he used to try, just as he used to wash the windows for her with no prompting, and clean out the mudroom, and toil in the kitchen making her favorite dessert of blueberry cobbler—such an American dessert. And he knew his mother's recipe so well he could cook the berries at just the right temperature and make the buttery crumble with the ease of a pastry chef. But years ago cobblers had gone the way of bell-bottoms and platform shoes.

Leticia had married Ted in 1970, after she had just turned twenty-four, imagining she had finally found someone to take care of her properly. After all, Ted was fifteen years older—mature and wise, she had reasoned, with a good job and a house already, and yes, he was divorced, but his first wife had left *him*, and Ted seemed like the kind of steady man who would never leave. Back then, that had been his charm and attraction.

Leticia and Ted had been married thirteen years now. Such an unlucky number. But perhaps the unlucky part about it was that she was still married to him at all.

Leticia followed Leopold out to the inn's parking lot.

"I should let you drive," he said.

"You are very funny."

"No, I mean it," he said. "I should teach you."

Leticia opened the passenger door and got in. The rental car smelled of stale cigarette smoke, a reminder of vices. Leticia rolled down the window and let the air wash her face with morning as they pulled away from the inn. Leopold kept pushing up his glasses at the bridge of his nose, even when they were not slipping down. Leticia had never before picked up on this particular habit he had, not that in the years they had known each other she hadn't observed other things about him: that he made jokes but forgot punchlines; that he had a receding hairline that reminded her of tidewater drifting out, leaving beachfront; and that he giggled instead of laughed, but only when he was tipsy. Leticia also knew the things Marta had told Leticia about him: Leopold clicked his jaw when he slept (it constantly awakened Marta), got stomachaches after eating strawberries or eggplant, and never drank coffee although he started work early and came home most nights after nine o'clock. Perhaps this last thing was because he and Marta had tired of each other years ago, but still, they fought as if it mattered, or at least he did. Marta preferred to play dead. In the car, Leticia noticed that when Leopold smiled, which he did every twenty seconds at Leticia even when they weren't in conversation, his teeth were perfectly straight and so much whiter than Ted's yellowed ones.

"Thanks for coming along," Leopold said, taking his eyes off the windshield for a moment to catch Leticia's gaze. "Did I make too much of a scene? I hope you didn't do this because you felt sorry for me."

"I did a little," she said. "But I also thought it could be fun, something different." He had such long sideburns, and stubbly cheeks. The only time she ever saw him unshaven was on vacation. She turned to the window and let the breeze haunt her face.

"Things okay with Ted?" Leopold asked.

"The same like always."

"Is that a good thing?"

It was a bold question, especially for Leopold. "You know Ted better than anyone else," she said.

"I suppose I do," Leopold said. "But he doesn't really confide. Does he to you?"

She yawned, already regretting joining Leopold and his game of questions. What had she been thinking? Marta was right: Leopold was tiresome.

"He does not talk to me, either—not like that," she said.

"Okay then," he said. He exited and clicked the turn signal to merge onto the highway. The others cars moved aside and let him in.

Leopold and Ted had started at the plant around the same time and risen through the ranks more or less at the same pace over the years. Now they were not only plant managers but golf partners, meeting on Saturday mornings and lunching afterward on bacon and cheese croissant sandwiches that Ted wished aloud that Leticia would make at home. The two men spent more time together just on that weekly golf outing than she spent alone with Ted in their waking moments over the course of a week. When Ted shuffled in from work, he retired to his home office and poured himself a drink from the decanter he kept on the antique mahogany table his mother had given him just before she died. Sometimes he sat in that office with his drink for a long time; other times he sank into the love seat in front of the small black-and-white television in the corner of the living room, where they'd briefly had a playpen. For two years, they had fought about where that television should go. He'd insisted on the living room, but Leticia wanted it banished to the den in the back of the house. She admitted that, yes, the den was somber with its dark panels, and it became humid in summers and frozen in winters, but she offered to buy him a fan for the sweltering temperatures and a space heater to break the chill.

"When we have a perfectly good room up front, with the exact right spot for it?" he said.

"Nothing about it is perfect," she said.

One night, more drunk than usual, he had yanked the front door open and bellowed from the stoop, "I want my TV! I want my TV!" His bathrobe fluttered in the evening wind. Leticia had given in—the only thing she could do to get him back inside.

Sitting in the car with Leopold, as she lifted her thick mass of hair and let the wind cool her neck, Leticia thought the television incident a little comical. Back then, she had cried for nearly a week. Most days now she kept the television on during the entire morning and afternoon, allowing *The Price is Right* and *Guiding Light* to drone on in the background so she could hear someone else's voice in the rooms that were more barren with every year.

Leopold waved his arms in front of him and then brushed off another cobweb sticking to his face. It appeared no other hikers had come through recently, at least from the size of the webs and their intricate outgoing patterns that spanned the path. Leopold insisted on being the one to walk in front, and he swiped the spiders' strings with a flail of his arms.

They had been walking for well over an hour, climbing higher. Sweat dripped down Leticia's face. She had worn white cotton pants, useless tennis shoes with thin soles, and a striped white and royal blue top with quarter-length sleeves and a buttonhole neckline, all the wrong things, really, for such a scorching day, on such a steep climb. She chided herself for this, for not having asked Leopold the right questions.

"Where does this lead?" Leticia asked.

"We're supposed to come to the summit."

They were climbing all the way to the top?

"It's supposed to have a spectacular view," he said.

"Of what?" Leticia asked.

"The great beyond."

Marta was right: Leopold could be theatrical. At times Marta had wondered aloud to Leticia whether Leopold was enough of a man. Marta made these kinds of offhand remarks while grinding coriander seeds or stirring a pot of soup and tossing in a dash of cumin—Marta never measured anything, claimed that teaspoons and measuring cups were all drudgery. "He was never very good at the whole sex thing," Marta told Leticia once. "He always struck me as unpracticed. What kind of man doesn't sow his seeds before marriage?"

Marta never made dinner on time: the men often had a cocktail in the Everharts' living room while Leticia sat on one of the black leather stools at Marta's kitchen counter, flipping through *McCall's* or *Good Housekeeping*, such American magazines even though Marta had only come to the States when she was eighteen, just as Leticia had.

"I think he has women issues," Marta said, dropping minced garlic into a bubbling pot.

Leticia wanted to ask Marta what she meant, but at the same time she felt embarrassed for Leopold, having his insecurities and intimacies thrown about. Maybe that's what all couples did when they had been married for over two decades like the Everharts. Leticia's mother had warned Leticia long ago to keep tight-lipped about everything, anything—*guárdate los secretos*—because once you gave away secrets, people would use them to steal other things from you.

Marta went on: "It's as if he is scared of his own manhood. And now, I've stopped wanting to bother with the whole thing. It's just tiresome, really. What about you and Ted?"

Leticia closed the magazine but continued staring at it, not lifting her hand from the back cover. "Ted and I, we are fine."

Marta whistled. "He must be a stallion, that one. He even drinks, and still he manages." Marta pointed with a wooden spoon at Leticia's face. "You're blushing. Such an innocent." Marta sashayed to the refrigerator. "I'll leave it alone for now, but I'll come back to it and find out your secrets, Leti." Marta was the only one of her friends who called Leticia by the nickname of her youth. It made Leticia feel young and foolish, the way her brothers had made her feel when they had teased her about her skinny body, thick untamable hair, sunken cheeks, and how she was just a girl and would therefore never amount to anything.

When Leticia was twenty-one and about to graduate from her American college, her mother had insisted—via several lengthy letters and one two-minute call—that Leticia meet Luis Villareal. He was a twenty-three-year-old mechanical engineering student pursuing his master's degree in a city forty-five miles away from Leticia's school. He was the son of Tío Paulo's boss, a man who owned one of the largest ranches in Chihuahua. Even though she did not want to, Leticia agreed to meet Luis. In her family, disobedience and defiance from a girl were unattractive and impossible.

On their first date, Luis brought Leticia a box of coconut candy and took her to an American diner, where they ordered hamburgers and Coca-Colas. He had a cowlick, and a dimple in his chin, and one tooth was covered in silver, but it was toward the back, a molar, so that Leticia only saw it when he laughed hard, opening his mouth wide and letting in the sky. On the drive home, he reached across the bench seat, grabbed her hand, and squeezed it. Leticia had thought it so forward that she yanked hers away. Still, she studied his profile when she thought he wasn't paying attention, and she deemed his nose rather noble. On their next date, sitting in the darkness of a movie theater watching *The Graduate,* she let him take her hand again and keep it. He had a callous on his thumb, and she could feel its roughness, but she focused on the smoothness of his palm.

Luis led Leticia to believe all he wanted was a good job and a family, and that seemed like enough to Leticia. Over the next few months, he took her out faithfully on Wednesday evenings. His weekend nights, he said, were dedicated to studying. In time, he pushed her to kiss him, and she let him, at first just small pecks, and later open-mouthed, the way she had heard other girls in her dormitory say they had done.

Only one boy had ever so much as looked at Leticia before, and this softened her view of Luis, made her wince less when he chewed ice from his drinks with his mouth open, when he dug a finger in his ear, when he smelled a little like a dirty sock when he sweated, which happened when he was nervous. Leticia spent a lot of time trying to make him less so. She wondered later if that is why she had not outwardly protested when, in the darkness of the back of his car, he had slid his hand beneath her skirt. It had all happened so fast, and she wanted to say no but had felt at fault for letting him kiss her so hard, for allowing him to brush his hands across her breasts. Afterward, he whisked her back to the dormitory, assuring her he was only in a rush because he did not want to drive back too late to his city. But a week later, he did not show, and two weeks later, she did not wait for him at the door of the dormitory, her purse clutched to her chest. Her mother had taught her to believe that if you wanted to make something vanish, you should speak of it less or not at all, so Leticia told no one about the cold leather in the back seat of the car, the buckle pressing into her shoulder, his palms pressing flat against hers.

After graduation, instead of taking the train back home to Mexico, in spite of her parents' protests, Leticia remained in the States, a country where she could remain invisible. She prayed for her parents' forgiveness, for the things they knew and the things they would never know. She got a job as a laboratory assistant in the very city, forty-five minutes away, where Luis lived—it had been her only offer—and she prayed she would not see him. The job paid just enough to cover rent for a tiny apartment that smelled of cat urine and had pencil scratches all along the walls. She cooked rice and boiled pinto and black beans, and she splurged on dark chicken meat when she was extra careful, if she did not go to the cinema and if she bought big bars of Octagon soap instead of the Dove beauty bars that the girls in school had used to scrub away their days.

She never saw Luis again, and she believed this to signify absolution for what had happened, for what she judged to have ultimately been her own sin.

Leopold was right: the view on top of Bald Mountain was spectacular, even though Leticia was exhausted. He pointed out the Sierras, Mount Diablo, and San Francisco Bay. Sitting on the brittle grass of the summit, Leopold offered Leticia a peach, which she politely declined. He withdrew a thermos of water and two granola bars from his backpack. When he had removed the pack from his shoulders, Leticia could see the wet trace of it on the back of his shirt, a shadow of what lay below.

"Aren't you hungry?" he asked.

She shook her head and lifted her face to the sun. Even though she was hot, she liked the feel of it.

"You sure?" he asked.

"I don't like to eat much for breakfast, but I did today."

"Oh, that's right," he said. "Usually it's just a cup of tea and half a cookie of some sort."

She raised her eyebrows.

He waved his hand with the granola bar in his clutch. "Ted told me."

"What else did he tell you?"

Leopold bit into the granola bar, chewed it, and swallowed. "That you love the Bee Gees, but only the songs from a few years back, like 'How Deep Is Your Love.' And you play it when he's not there. He finds the cassettes still in the stereo. Oh, yeah, and that you forget to turn off the stereo. He thinks you don't know how."

"I know how."

Leopold laughed. "And you hum in your sleep."

"That is not the truth."

"And you like to cook even when you're not hungry."

"Yes, yes," Leticia said. She lifted her face again to the sun, and she felt a warmth toward Leopold, flattered that he'd paid attention. Or was it Ted who had paid attention?

"He said he knows you miss Teddy Jr." *El nene*, her baby boy.

She opened her eyes. The sun burned.

"I'm sorry," Leopold said. "I shouldn't have—"

"It is fine, fine. So long ago." Nine years, two months, six days.

"No one should have to endure such things, Tici." No one had ever called her "Tici," except her grandmother, her *abuelita*.

Leticia pulled her knees to her chest and closed her eyes, lifting her face again, offering it up to the vast sky.

They hiked the rest of the way mostly in silence, Leticia trailing him by a few feet. They stood next to each other when he lost the way twice, and she moved closer to him than before, leaning in to see the lines of a map she could not figure out. He asked her which way she thought was right, and she considered and pointed but did not really know.

A week after the Everharts and the Smiths flew home to the Midwest from their wine country vacation, Leopold and Marta left again for a few days, this time to Florida to see their daughter sing in her sorority's annual talent show. Lucky for them since the gusts and gray air had shifted in and portended an early winter at home. Leticia wondered if their trip would be romantic, if they would hold hands sitting next to each other on chaise lounge chairs and drink fruity cocktails with miniature orange paper umbrellas. She had never seen them do such things, but perhaps they acted differently outside her presence.

Marta had asked Leticia to feed their cat, Thriller, in their absence. "I'm sorry Ted will have to drive you over here to do it."

"He will not mind," Leticia said.

"But I will," Marta said.

At the beginning of their courtship, Ted had made a big show of opening Leticia's door and being at her beck and call whenever she needed to go somewhere, even if it was to pick up something small like cotton swabs or lotion. Now, sometimes, he refused to take her where she asked to go, instead driving her to someplace else that he considered "just as good," which meant closer, or he pushed off her errand a day or two until he felt like taking her. There was a time when they had argued about such things, but now Leticia resigned herself to whatever his schedule allowed. She wondered if Leopold ever drove Marta to places when Marta did not feel like driving herself. Did Marta *ever* feel like not driving herself?

Leticia found herself thinking entirely too much about the Everharts' trip, conjuring up images of them nuzzling and kissing, neither of which she had ever seen them do. To keep her mind occupied, she forced herself into house projects.

"Leti, you okay?" Ted asked when he found her speckled with paint flecks in *el nene*'s former room. She was painting the blue walls yellow.

"Of course, why wouldn't I be?" she said, not putting her brush down, only turning her head to see Ted standing in the doorway to the bedroom, suit jacket flung over his shoulder. He had not ventured onto the plastic sheet she had spread all over the floor. It bore puddles of paint.

"Looks like a wild animal got loose in here," he said.

She was barefoot, and her hair drifted in front of her face. "I am fine, Ted. Go on." She resumed her work, which kept her focused for two days straight.

On Monday the phone rang as Leticia swept the kitchen floor. *It must be Marta*, she thought, since the Everharts should have returned the night before.

"Tici, it's me."

"Leopold?"

He sounded out of breath. "Can you hear me?" he asked.

She could but barely. "From where are you calling me?"

"I'm at Perkins on 8th Avenue, at a pay phone."

She looked at her watch: 9:25 a.m. He should be at work. "Is everything okay?" Had there been some sort of accident? "Is it Ted?"

"It's just me," he said. "Nothing's wrong."

She exhaled and loosened her grip on the phone. His labored breathing reminded her of the sound an LP makes when it gets to the end.

"I know I'm not supposed to be calling you," he said, "but I'm calling anyway."

Leticia imagined her mother scowling.

"Is it okay that I'm calling?" he asked. "Because if it's not okay, I'll hang up now. Just tell me what you want me to do."

In the corner of the kitchen, the clothes washer began to rock and bang against the floor, its balance thrown off by too many towels, too many sheets. "I don't know," she said.

"Let me come over so we can talk."

"No."

"Okay," he said. "I understand."

Leticia walked to the washer and lifted the lid, and the spinning made a wheezing sound as it came to a halt. "Which Perkins?"

"I'll send a taxi for you," Leopold said.

"The neighbors will see." She shut the lid again on the now-silent machine.

Leopold told her what city bus to take. The closest stop was half a mile away. She had taken the bus only once, years ago, but the memory of the old man who had sat behind her and slurred at her had stopped her from trying again.

"I'll order a pot of coffee," he said. "I'll wait as long as it takes."

The day swelled with gusts, nippy and full of trouble, the wind picking up dry leaves and tossing them back to ground. It was a day yearning for warmer West Coast weather to arrive and relieve everyone, for a while or maybe longer.

On the bus, Leticia held onto the silver rail that spanned the back of the seat in front of her. The bus chugged along the city blocks, the driver shouting out street names just before he hit the brakes, everyone lurching forward. People hurried, sometimes shoving past each other in the getting on and getting off. A woman across the narrow aisle kept sneezing into her sleeve.

Leticia's neck was damp, as was her back against the seat. She counted blocks but lost track. She crossed and uncrossed her legs. She fiddled with a ring she wore on her right hand, a thin gold band that had belonged to her *abuelita*, the woman who had taught Leticia how to count money, how to braid her own hair, how to know when to pick a prickly pear—when the green had disappeared and the fruit was blushed in red—and to understand that the tiny, nearly invisible cactus bristles were more dangerous than the long spines that were apparent to even the heedless observer. Leticia rolled the ring around and around her finger. The ring had loosened on her finger in recent years; sometimes it fell off. Leticia always managed to find it: in the dust below the nightstand, in the soapy water sloshing in the kitchen sink, or wedged between two couch pillows. What other things had she lost over the years but never found, things she had always presumed were unfindable? Was it possible she had been wrong, or not looked hard enough?

The stop was coming closer, and Leticia pulled on the string that rang the bell. The brakes squealed in recognition, and the bus slowed, screeched, and edged to the curb. The door shot open with a thwap. The driver looked up in his rearview mirror. The bus engine gave its low grumble.

"Who rang the bell?" the driver shouted.

Leticia did not rise from her seat. Wintry air wafted around her legs, billowed like smoke. She gripped the silver rail and stood. She shuffled to the front. "Is this the 8th?"

"Yep," the driver said.

"Oh, I-I think I was wrong."

"Where you wantin' to go?"

"I think I left something at home," she said.

"Then sit down, lady. And don't ring the bell unless you know what the hell you're doing."

Leticia made her way back to her seat. The bus door flapped shut. Leopold would probably be eating toast by now, buttering it slowly, or he would be holding the coffee mug, warming his hands. He would be sitting in a booth, facing the entrance. He would wait longer than he should. When she did not come, he would call the house to find out what had happened, and she would want to pick up, but she would not.

Hours later, a car pulled into the Smiths' driveway. Leticia got up from the kitchen table, where she had been eating a cold, unbuttered piece of toast and sipping on Sanka. She walked into the living room and peered out the window: there was the Everharts' Lincoln Town Car. The room tilted and swayed beneath and around Leticia. She clutched the back of the couch.

Inside the car, Marta was reaching over to the passenger seat to grab something. She threw open the car door and strode toward Leticia's front stoop. Marta's face looked hardened in the bitter wind, and she tucked her chin into the collar of her purple wool coat.

"What's wrong?" Marta asked when Leticia opened the front door.

Leticia shook her head and drew her velour housecoat tighter against her body. When she had gotten home from her bus ride, she had stripped down to her underwear and thrown her clothes directly in the wash. Toast crumbs clung to the velour.

"Here. For you." Marta held out a loaf of zucchini bread. "Your favorite. I made it early this morning. Thank you for taking care of Thriller."

"Oh," Leticia said.

"Aren't you going to let me in?"

Leticia did not want to. "Of course."

"You don't look so well, Leti dear. You sure you're alright? Do you have a temperature?"

Leticia nodded to Marta's silver sedan. "Did he buy that for you?"

Marta clucked at her. "Such a strange question. Of course not. *We* bought it for me. Now, Leti darling, I've just made a decision. You're going out with me right now. It's time to teach you a thing or two. Let's get you inside and find you something warm to wear instead of that dreadful housecoat. Doesn't Ted buy you anything nice?"

The two women sat in the Lincoln Town Car between two white parking lines in the high school parking lot. "You have to adjust your mirrors first." Marta pointed to the rearview and then side mirrors. Leticia had seen Ted do this when they borrowed someone else's car or rented one. Their own car was always adjusted to Ted.

Marta told Leticia to keep both hands on the wheel, to turn on the headlights at dusk and when it rained, and she showed Leticia how to click on the turn signal and said to use it even when only passing a car, even if other drivers did not, and then she added, "Even if Ted tells you later not to bother." Marta explained how the right foot switched back and forth from accelerator to brake pedal, how the left foot remained still. "Just like a marriage," Marta said with a chuckle. "One person seems unimportant but actually provides all the stability, don't you agree?" She directed Leticia to turn the key and start up the engine. "Go on then. It will not do you any good to have the lesson only in your head."

Leticia moved the car out of park and stepped on the gas pedal too hard. The car lurched and she braked, but she was a quick learner, and Marta did not have to correct her, for Leticia would never make the same mistake twice. Leticia propelled the car forward, steadily this time, with just enough gas, and she made her way easily around the parking lot in the sedan that at first glance had seemed too big for a couple whose child no longer lived at home but now seemed just large enough to contain them.

The padded steering wheel was smooth and solid in Leticia's hands. She liked how even the slightest shift of the wheel turned the vehicle in a new direction. Ted had explained to her, more than once, how cars had either good or bad responsive handling, but she had not understood what that meant until now.

Leticia drove around the lot twelve times before Marta said, "Good enough. Now it is time."

It wasn't until she was driving down a street, Marta clapping, that Leticia understood all the reasons she had not learned how to drive a car: she had been scared of the power of metal and engine combined, had believed that she would not understand the street signs, or that she would jerk the car in and out of lanes, or that the car would break down and she would not know why. Her concerns about her potential weaknesses had obscured her strengths, had overshadowed her own ability to handle any number of things, the ability she had been sure of when she had rented that urine-smelling apartment, when although it smelled, she knew she could pay the rent, and though the windows had to be tugged hard to shut and open, she knew she had the muscle and would learn the tricks. Leticia had not anticipated knowing the tricks to driving, had underestimated her own capacity to pick up on signs, to understand, intuitively, how much gas to give and when to tap the brakes, and when to slam them.

Many years ago, Ted had taken Leticia and *el nene*, swaddled in her arms, on summer Sunday drives through the city. Back then, she had sensed the season's impending end, the way the leaves were beginning to slip from the branches and cling to the earthen floor. As they had driven through the city, they had passed the ice cream store with its swirling candy cane, Katzinger's diner with its neon blue sign, and Buck's pharmacy that stayed open all night in emergencies, where Buck could be roused from home to come and unlock the glass door with its jingling bell and let them in if a prescription could not wait until morning. He would rub his bald head and lumber to the back, and they would wait hunched by the malt station, all milk and ice cream put away, and listen to the sound of pills dropping onto metal dish for the counting, the rolling of a paper bag. Back then she had thought of these sounds as soothing. She had imagined these places, this life, would last.

"You're a perfect driver," Marta said. "I can't believe how well you have picked up on this, so quickly."

It felt to Leticia as if she had been driving for years. "Should we go now on the highway?" Leticia was already clicking on her turn signal and moving toward the exit ramp.

Marta laughed.

"Can we roll down the windows?"

"Why are you asking me?" Marta said and rolled down hers. She put her face to the biting wind and let out a whoop. Leticia laughed and then joined her. She had not yet learned how to whoop as Marta had. Leticia's whoop was flimsy and meek, but she found she had another, and another, and together they flapped out of the windows and into the gray horizon, for nothing could contain them any longer.

HANK'S GIRL

The next morning, Franny spent too much time explaining to Mrs. Poughkeepsie what had happened to her eye. Franny had peeked from behind the curtains to make sure no one was coming down the lane before running in her robe to fetch the newspaper at the end of the driveway, but Mrs. Poughkeepsie appeared out of nowhere, ambling toward Franny and pointing at her with the tip of her black umbrella. Franny proceeded to string sentences together into a rope that lengthened yet tightened, going on and on about how last night Hank's dog had to pee so Franny put its leash on and went outside and thought she had a good grip but then the dog tugged her too fast into the front yard—"It must have really had to go," she heard herself saying, her voice high and nasally—and the yard was dark and she banged into a branch on the old oak tree and, "oh, if only Hank had cut that one branch down," then she regretted saying that, even involving Hank, "but he has been so busy with his new job," she added, "working so hard, such a good provider, my Hank," and Mrs. Poughkeepsie smiled and nodded, as all the neighbors did when Franny spoke about Hank, for they had been giving the newlyweds jams and jellies and sweet bread, so many rolls and loaves that Franny at first tried to keep up eating them, but Hank told her that was ridiculous, so Franny eventually wrapped them in foil and pushed them into the back of the freezer to forget them. Franny went on too long to Mrs. Poughkeepsie about how this morning

Hank had helped her put ice on her eye, and it was true, he had touched it with one finger to see how bad it was, brushed her hair back from her face with the other hand while she sat on the closed toilet seat. She didn't tell Mrs. Poughkeepsie that last part, or that he had run out of words by then, how quiet he was, like the calm surface of water after it has swallowed something, how eventually he handed the bag of ice to her and mumbled he must go to work, even though it was only seven o'clock, an hour earlier than when he usually left. He had bent down to kiss her cheek and then paused, patting her on the top of the head instead.

"I've gotta go, Mrs. Poughkeepsie," Franny heard herself saying. "So much to do!" Though she could not think of what.

"No one loves you as much as I do, Francine," Hank had said before leaving. "You should know that by now. No one."

The dog was barking now, lunging against the storm door.

When Lily called at quarter 'til eleven, as she often did while her students were at lunch in the cafeteria, Franny thought of Hank and wasn't going to answer, but she couldn't help herself. For the next few minutes, she went on too long about how she must have had too much coffee, her hands were shaking.

"Shaking?" Lily asked with a mouthful of bologna sandwich. Lily always took a bologna sandwich to work, just as she had done in school.

"I didn't mean that much," Franny said. She felt nauseous.

The dog was sitting at Franny's feet, gazing up at her while she held on to the phone. The dog whimpered, always wanting something, but Franny never knew what. Through the receiver, Franny could hear teenagers shouting and laughing, and the clattering of trays on tables, for Lily always used the pay phone in the hallway closest to the cafeteria so she could keep an eye on them, even though she wasn't on lunch duty except for Mondays.

(Franny pictured Lily's tanned face, her wispy row of brown bangs, the freckles on her cheeks like constellations—the exact way Lily looked last summer after the week she and Franny had spent alone at the cabin on Songbird Pond.)

"You sure you don't have the flu?" Lily asked. The girls had been nearly inseparable for seventeen years, since first grade when they rode the school bus together and big Bo Benson had pinched Franny, and Lily clocked him on the shoulder with her plaid metal lunch box. Bo Benson had died last year in Vietnam. Who was next?

"I'm fine," Franny said.

"You don't sound fine."

"It was a long night."

"What was so long about it? The fact of his existence?"

Lily had never approved of Hank, so Franny told Lily about the dog, but this time she tripped over a fallen branch, and Hank helped her with her eye that night, did not wait until the morning when his hands were steady.

"So your tripping is what made it a long night?" Lily asked.

Franny didn't know how to answer.

"Was the fall that bad?" Lily was now asking. "Did it leave a mark?"

"Not really," she said, touching her eye the way Hank had (but it was Lily's hand she felt, soft and certain). Franny shooed the dog away.

"Can't Hank take you to the doctor? What good is being married to him if he can't even do that?"

"Hank said it's nothing."

The dog was licking its paws, and Franny swatted it to make it stop.

At twelve o'clock, Franny didn't want to walk the dog around the block, as Hank had instructed her to do when they first married, as she always did now. She let the dog out the back door, and it sprinted around the rose bushes, galloped toward the fence, peed on Franny's geraniums and then began digging up her bearded irises, tearing open the lawn. "Stop, stop!" Franny waved her arms wildly at the door. She clamped a hand over her mouth, startled by the loudness of her own voice. What if the neighbors heard? Hank always said to hush.

The dog stopped, its ears perked. It stared at her.

"Come here," Franny said in the loudest whisper she could muster. "Come here right now or else . . ." But she could not think what she could possibly do, and the dog resumed its digging.

Franny made too many wrong turns driving to the Piggly Wiggly at one o'clock. Hank had told her a million times how to get there— he'd admonished her just three days ago for not writing down his directions. Franny would never make it to the Piggly Wiggly if she did not straighten up, become more like the wives with bobs and hair parted down the very middle, with short skirts and stockings, with purses hanging down from their arms like anchors. She pulled over and retrieved the map from the glove box and smoothed it flat on her lap, but even then the city intersections all looked like thin crosses, row after row, and Franny stuffed the map back into the glove box and kept driving until she saw the store with its big P and W letters. As she made a left turn into the Piggly Wiggly parking lot, she almost ran into another car—how could she not have seen it coming toward her in the other lane?—and she lurched into a space and was sweating now, parked so far from the store's glass doors.

Someone rapped their knuckles on the window, and Franny jumped in her seat. "You okay?" a man asked when she rolled down her window just a crack. "Saw you nearly plow into that guy." He was wearing a black-and-white-striped knit hat, though it was hot out, and his beard was like her father's, long and gray and twisted at the end.

"I-I'm fine," she said.

He leaned down, hands on his denim knees. He pointed through the glass. "You got a shiner."

"No it's not." She checked herself in the rearview mirror. Her makeup had sweated off. "I bumped into a kitchen cupboard last night—it was dark, and I tripped over my husband's dog, well, it's our dog now, of course, I just mean I sometimes forget to remember the dog is there. I can be so clumsy." She touched the spot; it was soft and sore. She forced herself to smile at him. "I'm fine, sir, thank you."

He stood up, squinted into the sun, swatted a fly away. "Okay, lady."

Franny washed and waxed all the kitchen appliances that afternoon from two to four o'clock. It was Wednesday after all. She started with the long face of the yellow refrigerator, then the matching dishwasher and, last, the companion yellow stove. Franny scrubbed its eyes out, too. Her hands, red and raw, were barely shaking now.

Franny's mother called at quarter past four, as she often did to see what Franny was planning for dinner. "He loves my pot roast recipe," her mother said. "Is that what you're making?"

Franny had meant to, but she had not gone into the Piggly Wiggly after all, had not picked up a rump roast or papery onions or parsnips or hard, white potatoes. Instead, she had driven home slowly and carefully, looking for the landmarks Hank always emphasized: the Fortune Cookie, Suds & Duds, Eddie's Pizzeria. "I'm making Salisbury steaks," Franny said.

Her mother clucked her tongue. "Frozen dinners? Heavens."

Franny looked down at her freshly mopped linoleum floor, saw paw prints by the door and stretched the phone cord until she could reach the spots to wipe them with a wet rag. "They're Swansons," Franny said. "Hank likes those. He said that's okay."

"But honey, you haven't even been married a year."

At quarter 'til five, Lily phoned again, which she almost never did, for Hank sometimes came home early, and whenever he found them talking he made it a point to use the newfangled, motor-roaring trash compactor in the kitchen, making it impossible for Franny to hear Lily. The school hallway where Lily worked must have lain vacant because Franny heard no yelling or laughing.

"Detention is over," Lily said.

Franny swallowed. She shut her eyes.

"Are you still there?" Lily asked.

The kitchen smelled of bleach, too strong, as if nothing could ever get clean enough. "I'm here," she whispered, sure Lily had not heard her.

The dish towel hung limp over the back of a chair.

"You don't belong with him," Lily said. "Come home."

(The memory broke, like stone tossed into silver water. "You don't belong with him," Lily had said last summer just before Franny married Hank, the same summer Lily and Franny spent their week at the cabin on Songbird Pond. Lily's parents had purchased the two-room cabin in 1954. It had no hot water but plenty of chilly-bump cold, and a toilet that required a bucket for flushing, and a weather-beaten front door with a lock that did not work, that Lily claimed never had. Lily's parents didn't believe in shoulds; they let things be. The cabin was eighty-two miles from Franny's and Lily's hometown and just enough miles from nowhere that Franny and Lily did not hear the voice of anyone else for seven days, just the calling and answering of geese, loons, owls. If you walked fifty steps from the front porch, you came to a pond surrounded by wisps of cattail, rush, and sedge, a place that felt like nowhere else, where you could become lost or someone else or the person you were always meant to be.

In the cabin, Lily cracked open eggs and sizzled them into sunny-side. She poured corn bread batter into an old cast-iron skillet and made the concoction rise to moist and salty-sweet. She melted chocolate and heated milk and stirred them together into cocoa meant to be sipped on a cool night, held in a cup with both hands.

Hanging on the cabin walls and lying across the bed were gingham quilts, all hand-sewn by Lily's now-dead grandmother, Ada, who had slowly lost her eyesight and was declared blind by age thirty-two. "You don't need eyes to understand someone's threads and fabric edges," Ada had told Lily, and Lily had recounted to Franny during those seven days on Songbird Pond, when they had swum until their skin turned golden, slept against each other until daylight broke through windows, and talked until silence meant more than words.

This memory and all its petals opened then closed for Franny, like something with the will to bloom despite the immediate bite of an early but expected frost.)

At quarter 'til six, Franny dragged the hard, blue Samsonite suitcase from under the bed and across the Tang-orange carpet. She opened the drawers of the highboy and lifted out her stack of underwear, careful not to muss Hank's side of the drawer, for now they shared every single drawer instead of having separate ones. Franny closed the drawer and sat on the edge of their double bed. The dog came in and curled up beside her feet. Franny smoothed her skirt over and over. She had spent too much time explaining to her mother why she wanted to come home for a visit but had not mentioned Lily or Lily's call, for Franny's mother had never liked Lily, said she should be wearing dresses instead of all those pants. "Hank's been so busy at work," Franny had said on the phone to her mother, "so so busy, and working nights and even weekends, and it's important he make a good impression, and he needs to focus, and I just feel like a big distraction right now, and I don't want him worrying about me—I can be so clumsy, you know how clumsy I am, I've always been clumsy, and I did the stupidest thing last night, so stupid you are just gonna laugh that I even did it."

"You're not driving in the dark. You'll have to wait 'til morning. Did Hank say it was okay for you to go?"

"We haven't really—"

"Who will feed him?" her mother asked.

"I-I can leave meals for him," Franny said.

"Oh," her mother said. "Not more frozen dinners, I hope."

The dog was standing on its hind legs, scratching at the bedroom door.

◆◆◆

When Hank came home, it was past nine, and his shirt was rumpled, his tie half undone. He was not wearing his suit jacket. He held out a box of Brach's Contessa Chocolates. "I love you so much," he said. "You know that, right?" The box was pink and red and falling open.

"What's this?" she asked. Her stomach turned once, twice, like a dog chasing its tail.

"What, you don't want them?" he said.

She reached for them. "No, it's just—"

"Because I can take them back." He held them high.

"I want them," she said. She reached.

He held them higher.

"Stop it," she said. "It's not a game."

He lowered his arms. "I know," he said. "I'm sorry. At least give me a smile."

She offered him a perfunctory one.

"That's better," he said, handing over the box. "Your mother called me."

"She did?" The room smelled of wet dog, though the dog was nowhere in sight.

"Your mother doesn't like it when you go back. I don't either," he said. "You should be here."

"I just need some time."

"Did Lily put you up to this?"

Her hands felt moist, the box of chocolates sticky.

He rubbed his eye with his fist. "Don't, Franny. You don't need Lily. She doesn't know you like I do."

Franny didn't know who anyone was or had ever been. "You won't even know I'm gone," she said.

He took the box of chocolates from her and laid them on the edge of the coffee table. He put his arms around her. "Please," he whispered, "I need you. I've always needed you. I thought you needed me. Your parents think we're perfect together. Don't you? I promise to make you happy, but I can't make you happy if you won't let me. Please."

He held her against him, his shirt smelling faintly of Lucky Strikes, her father's favorites, and she closed her eyes and nodded into Hank's shirt.

"Good," he said into her hair. "Good." He squeezed her once before letting her go.

He pulled at his tie and flung it off. He strode toward the kitchen. "Where's my girl?" he asked. "She outside?"

HOUSE ON FIRE

When I get home, Daniela is humming again, eulogizing her day. God I love the sound of it even when she picks annoying, stupid songs like "I'm Proud to Be an American" or "God Bless the USA." She likes all the patriotic tunes that rednecks croon on the radio, though she's not from here, but I love her for how she can't tell what's crap and what isn't. It's as if she thinks that nothing in this country can go wrong or turn ugly or bad, as if even the toilets— which she has to clean every day, dozens and dozens at the motel where she works—were rimmed in gold she just can't see yet, not until she has scrubbed the grime away. Not that she ever says that. But sometimes you know everything about a person by what they don't say. If you looked at me right now, you'd see I've had a day, the kind that follows you even when you've tried to outrun it.

Daniela glances up at me before I say I'm home. She smiles. I wait for that smile all morning and afternoon, not the closed-mouth smile she gives me when she is really thinking about something else, but the smile I love—open-mouthed, so I can see the slight gap between her two front teeth, a gap that reminds me of the small spaces in the world where we let only a few people in. It's that smile that pulls me through the days of drudgery, pulls me like a string from lost to found, pulls me as I schlep people in my old minivan from ranches to duplexes to bungalows that need new water heaters and have cracks in their foundations but houses—despite defects and bad fixes and crumbling—that represent possibility to people who need it most. When people buy a place from me, they're seeking salvation. People find me by word-of-mouth, as if I am some sort of deep secret they must whisper to each other. And then there are *their* secrets, which they hand over to me, sometimes in bundles, like Monopoly money— useless in the real world. Everyone has long, tiresome stories that they want to tell me about their one-night stands, divorces, settlements, addictions, recoveries, and the worst—it is always the worst—about the people they love but can't be with for whatever stupid reason that never ends up being because of war or heroics but because humans are plain old foolish with their idiotic, bleeding hearts. No one knows what they want until it's too damn late.

I just want to sell houses and make some money for Daniela. Everything I do now is for Daniela. My ex-wife, Miriam, would probably say that everything I *used* to do was never enough for her, but I'm not asking Miriam, especially not today.

"You hungry?" Daniela gestures toward the card table we scored from the garage sale our neighbor had when her husband left her for his dental hygienist. We even got the husband's cat, orange and fat, for two dollars. Our neighbor was allergic but had put up with the animal because she loved her husband. Oh the things we give in to for love. Daniela is insane about the cat, named him Bambi for God knows what reason. Maybe because Bambi lost his mother the way Daniela did by coming to this country four years ago when she was twenty-two. Or maybe because Daniela thinks Bambi is an American classic. But if a cat named Bambi makes her happy, so be it, even if the stupid cat scratches the legs of my dad's old desk, taking off all the veneer. It doesn't matter. It's still the desk where I'm gonna write a book one day.

Daniela has folded up paper towels into compact squares as napkins on the card table, and she's set out some plasticware next to two mismatched melamine plates, from that same garage sale. They're nicer than the paper plates we used in the first few months we were together, but I didn't care then—still don't—about what I had, only what I didn't. I got nothing from my divorce, not that I can blame Miriam for that. I told her to keep it all. And Daniela, well, she says that having me is enough. Okay, she doesn't *say* that, but it's understood.

I'm hungry for everything and nothing. Daniela makes it easy to forget the hunger for nothing.

♦♦♦

Daniela wants the lights off when we have sex, so afterward, I fumble around for the lamp switch and get up and flip on the air conditioning unit and then slip back into bed. We try not to use the AC because the damn thing costs too much, like everything else, but tonight I'm feeling like I want to live more lavishly than usual, pretend I can spare a dime or two. It's because of the call I got from Gary.

"I have to go to a funeral tomorrow night," I tell Daniela when I have my arm around her again. Her shoulder feels like a doorknob. An opening. A closing.

She does not look at me with that pinched expression she often has. She just waits.

"Yeah," I say. "Someone died that I used to work with."

Daniela doesn't ask anything. She rarely does, and anyway I usually fill in her silences with answers to the questions I know she wants to ask. This time, I don't. It's Miriam's dad who died. And I'm not lying to Daniela: he *is* someone I worked with. Frank gave me my first real estate agent job, even paid for my real estate classes and license, but of course I was married to his daughter at the time. Gary, my former brother-in-law, is the one who called and told me the news earlier today. It kicked me in the balls, if you want to know the truth, but I don't know why—it's not like Frank and I have even talked in the last couple of years. Gary sounded bad, too, but he had more of a right to it. He's still in the family, married to Miriam's older sister, Anne Marie. I say older sister as if Miriam has a younger sister, too, which she doesn't, because if you have a sister like Anne Marie, one is more than plenty. Anyway, Gary didn't exactly invite me to the funeral, but it was implied. Everything about our conversations is always implied, as if we can't say the words directly to one another about what we really want or mean, but who the hell can?

Daniela rises from the bed. She likes to smoke after sunset, after sex, after a hot bath, after reading a letter from home, and after we come back from playing bingo at the community center, which I absolutely hate doing—the bingo part, not the coming home. I hate it when she smokes, too, but it's her only vice—and damn if I didn't used to do it back in the day—and anyway, I don't want to be the type of person who tries to change the one he loves. "You gonna go have a smoke?" I ask.

She shakes her head. "You hungry?" she asks again, and it feels as if time has rewound, or stopped, or done something close to what I have always wanted, which is to begin again, to be brand-new, if not for me, then for Daniela.

Daniela gets toothaches every few weeks, but she refuses to see a dentist and refuses to take aspirin. Tonight is one of those nights when she holds an ice pack to her cheek but does not complain. She serves me dinner using her free hand.

Her favorite cooking ingredients are lemon juice, vinegar, sour cream—only rarely all together. She puts mayonnaise on everything. Tonight she has made zucchini pancakes. She serves them cold since it's so damn miserable out. I don't know how the hell she finds time to make dinner with her crappy job schedule, but she does.

I've never met a harder worker than Daniela, except for Miriam, but to Miriam everything came easy. She made a boatload for every hour she mediated clients' arguments. It's different when you make next to nothing but work your ass off anyway. Not that Daniela ever brags about long hours, high standards, punctuality. In fact, she won some award at work—housekeeping staff member extraordinaire or something like that—and didn't even bother to tell me about it. I was putting away her laundry in her dresser drawer, and the award was tucked in the back, behind her bras. When I asked her about it, asked when she had gotten the award, she walked out of the room, calling out behind her, "It was stupid."

Stupid is our favorite word—well, it was mine and now it's hers. We find uses for it everywhere. Her stupid boss with his stupid toupee and stupid bad breath. This stupid crap-ass apartment with its stupid painted-shut windows and stupid broken locks, all of which we rent for money that feels like extortion every time we hand it over to our stupid landlord with his stupid toothpick hanging out of his mouth. Sometimes when I say stupid, it makes Daniela laugh. When she laughs really hard, which isn't very often, she covers her mouth, and I pull her hand away, wanting to see that gap between her teeth, but then she always stops. Unlike me, Daniela uses the word stupid sparingly, and when she does, she crowds it with other words that make it sound nicer than it is. She'll say things like "it was only a stupid little mistake," as if the word is more about forgiveness and regret, or making something smaller than it really is.

Sometimes I worry I'm teaching her all the wrong words.

I want to be America for her. I want to be front porches with mountain views, and smooth-engine cars with leather seats and cargo space. I want to be swimming pools, mahogany guitars, brand-new bikes. I want to be a bottle of bourbon and a jar of salted, roasted cashews. I buy these for Daniela when I make a good sale—a two-story with a back deck, finished basement, master suite on the main level, granite countertops in the kitchen, good school district. Daniela is always surprised when I buy her things, as if no one has ever given her a gift. Maybe no one has. When I can't find cashews or Angel's Envy, I buy her other things she loves: wool socks, antique salt and pepper shakers, or buttons, all kinds, any kind, as if the world can't be kept enough together.

When I wake up, Daniela's not in bed. I can tell just from the silence (she grinds her teeth, when she can actually sleep). She has terrible insomnia, wakes up at every godforsaken sound, even a damn cricket, while I can sleep through a swarm of police sirens. Daniela usually gets up before I do—she has to report to the motel by 6:30 a.m., even on Saturdays—but it's only 4 a.m. now. I find her in the living room, tucked into the end of the couch all torn up by Bambi, who is curled in Daniela's lap. She's holding a letter, which she folds up when she sees me and shoves beneath her legs. She wipes her face with her sleeve.

"What is it?" I ask.

She shakes her head.

"It can't be nothing if you're crying."

She doesn't answer, and I stop asking because why the hell should I crowbar something out of her she doesn't want to share? I put my arm around her, and I think about all the big things even a small person can contain.

At the funeral, I sit in the back pew, hoping no one will really notice me. All of Frank's community—clients and colleagues and friends—knew me and Miriam when we were together, so I'm pretty sure they all knew when we split up. This city is too small to evade gossip, even though I live in the slummy part of it now, far from where Miriam and her flock live their suburban lives. Right before the service starts, Miriam glances back, too late for me to shrink down in the pew. But when she sees me, she gives me the smallest smile, something she has not done since we were married. My neck, my face—suddenly I'm a house on fire.

Sitting beside her is Marcus, big and bulky. Even his hair is too damn thick. There's just too much of it, of him. Marcus is the guy Gary told me Miriam's been seeing for a while now. Says they're already serious. Says he thinks Marcus is going to pop the question soon. Gary can't stand the guy. I asked Gary why, and he said, "Marcus has a God complex." Then Gary made a coughing sound. "Sorry, man, I didn't mean to offend you by . . . not sure if that was the Lord's name in vain or something."

I laughed. "You didn't offend me, and anyway, I'm not, you know . . ." Religious. Anymore. If I ever was.

"Oh. Okay. Right," he says.

Marcus has his big thuggy arm around Miriam, like she's his possession. And maybe she is. Maybe that's what she wants now. What do I know about what she wants these days? Gary says Marcus hates that Miriam spends so much time with her family but that Marcus pretends to like Gary and Anne Marie when he sees them, makes jokes and slaps Gary on the back like they're old buddies. Gary says Miriam started seeing Marcus after her dad had his second heart attack six months ago. She met him online, from out of town— I don't know, something weird like that. Says Marcus wants Miriam to stop practicing mediation altogether, to stay at home and raise kids as soon as they have them.

"Isn't that what she wants, too?" I asked Gary. When we were together Miriam was desperate to have a kid. It was all she talked about sometimes, like that was the last chance for me to finally up and give her something of worth, and if I failed in that like I did everything else, well, then . . .

"I don't know what Miriam wants anymore," Gary says, which means he does, he just doesn't want to admit it.

The service goes on and on. There's a minister, of course, because Frank was a devout Presbyterian, unlike his two daughters, who slept in on Sundays and prayed to the goddess of yoga pants. The Presbyterians, at least his kind, are not into the damn-you-to-hell stuff, which for a while I wanted, craved, needed. Well, not the hell stuff—I had plenty of that—but the salvation. Maybe I just wanted someone besides Miriam to kick me in the ass and tell me to do something, anything, with my life. I guess it worked because here I am with my own business and the headaches to prove it.

Eventually, at the funeral, Anne Marie gets up and gives a three-minute speech about how great her dad was and how generous, which she should be saying because if it weren't for his money then she couldn't afford to raise five freakin' kids and eat anything besides rice and beans and use a rain barrel to flush the damn toilet. I look through the whole program and am surprised that Miriam isn't going to eulogize her dad at all. She's a hell of a lot more articulate than Anne Marie, more level-headed, more poised and together. But the whole time that Anne Marie talks, Miriam hangs her head down— and Miriam isn't the type to hang her head down about anything. We lost our unborn baby, and she didn't even shed a tear, just got pissed off at me, like it had all been some sort of test I flunked.

The fact that her head is hanging down tells me her dad's death is going to kill her. Everyone tells you that grief and hard times make you stronger, but that's not true. They make you weaker and smaller, make it so that you look at everyone else through your cloud of grief and wish that they were dead instead.

After the service, there's a gathering at Gary and Anne Marie's place. Gary told me about it ahead of time, and though he didn't exactly invite me, I got that it was okay to come by. It's already late, but I want to pay my respects to Miriam. I know I owe Frank a lot for what he did for me, including that he didn't run me out of the city when I started a real estate business that competed with his. Well, it didn't really compete with his. Frank had a specialty in the upper echelons of society while I specialize in the bottom.

There's a huge crowd at the house, people crammed into every room and corner holding drinks and mini plates full of crackers and cheese and shit, like this is a party. And maybe it is. Frank probably would've liked that, at least a little, even though he wouldn't have admitted it. Gary and Anne Marie's kids are running around like maniacs, screaming and chasing each other. The oldest one, who must be about ten now, is playing with a cell phone. Probably trying to find someone to call to get her the hell out of here. Their house was always like this, full of chaos. Miriam both hated and loved it.

"Hey, asshole," Anne Marie says to me when I almost walk by her in the living room. She's sitting on the couch, blouse popped open, breast-feeding her fifth child—five too many, if you ask me—where everyone can see.

"Hey, Bogey," Gary appears, extending a hand to me. "Awfully nice of you to come." I always did like ol' Gary, if for no other reason than because, God bless him, he's as devoted to Anne Marie as a dog is to digging up a cat turd. He's never left her despite the fact that she is a piece of work. He's solid, good as gold. Gary was the closest thing to a brother I ever had. After Miriam and I split up, Gary and I got together a couple of times for drinks, only I don't think Gary told either sister he had done so. He always knew how to play it cool.

"I won't stay long," I say to him. "I promise."

"Stay as long as you like," Gary says. "You know you're always welcome here."

"No he's not," Anne Marie says, not even remotely under her breath.

"I'm sorry about your dad," I say to her.

Anne Marie doesn't answer.

"Want something to drink?" Gary thumbs toward the kitchen. "I can get you something, or you know where the good stuff is."

I shake my head. "I came to see Miriam."

"She isn't here," says Anne Marie.

"I think I saw her go out back," Gary says.

"Yeah? You sure?" I ask.

He pats me on the arm. "I'm sure."

The moon is cut in half. There's just enough light from it and the back deck that I can see Miriam at the far end of the garden, next to the fountain Gary and I installed years ago. She's smoking, and I move toward the glow.

"Whoa," I say as I get closer. Miriam refused to smoke with me when we were together—just hassled me about it. "Never thought I'd see this."

She looks at me, unmoving, still holding her cigarette. Her eyes are vacant lots.

"Hey," I say. "I was just kidding. You can smoke if you want."

"Marcus would kill me if he knew," she says. "Want one?"

"Not anymore."

"You used to love these."

And it's true, I did, but I gave them up for her. Resented it, too, at least for a while. "Didn't know you knew how to do this," I say.

"I smoked some of yours back in the day. You used to leave a pack on my bedside. I got curious."

"You joking?"

She shakes her head.

"Why the hell did you keep harping on me to quit then?" I ask.

"Because I knew if you didn't, I wouldn't either." She exhales, blowing smoke just above my head.

"Wow. Thanks for that."

"There were a lot of things I didn't tell you that I probably should have. I used to think secrets could be scattered, that they could just drift away if we let them." Then she says, "Is this how you felt, Bogey? Is this how it was?"

And I know she's talking about when my dad died, six years ago, and the nights I smoked pot after she went to bed, how I lost my job, the years I just sat there. "Yeah," I say. "Probably."

She nods, but I wonder if she really does get it, or if she just doesn't want to be reminded of our past. "I'm really sorry," she says, like I'm the one who's lost everything.

I sit down on one of the stumps left back here after Gary cut down all the big ash trees on the property because of the bore that was invading the area. Better to go ahead and chop them down than watch them wither was what he said back then. But now I wonder.

"How's that girlfriend of yours?" Miriam asks.

"Great," I say. "How's ol' Marcus?"

She flicks ashes into the grass. "I'm surprised you know who he is."

"Gary says you two are getting married."

She raises her eyebrows, and I realize that I've given Gary's and my secret away—that he and I are still talking—but Miriam doesn't say anything, just keeps smoking and then takes the stump next to mine. And we sit there like that, not saying a word, and it feels so different than all the times we were married and not talking and it felt like suffocation.

"I had a dream last night," she says.

"Yeah?"

"I was twenty-two again. You were there, my dad was there, even Chigger was there, only he was still a pup," she says. "He peed on your shoes."

"That's symbolic," I say.

"He always peed on your shoes."

"But never on yours."

"Right," she says. "So, I woke up thinking I was twenty-two again and in that double bed. Remember the one I had when I lived on 19th? It sloped on one side and smelled like—"

"Mothballs. I fell off of it twice. Of course I remember."

She smiles. "I'd forgotten about that." She takes another drag from her cigarette. "I thought that's where I was this morning."

"Maybe you were, in a way." As soon as I say it, I get that sick feeling in my stomach I used to get when I was a kid and had eaten too much sugar or stolen something that I wasn't supposed to even know about. Still, the feeling doesn't stop me from saying, "Maybe I was there, too."

Through the back French doors, people mill about inside the house, people who've overloaded their plates with food and who are trying to keep it all from sliding off or toppling over.

"You didn't have to come," Miriam says. "So thank you for that."

"I loved Frank."

"He loved you. Even at the end."

"Yeah?" I say.

"He pretended he was mad at you," she says, "but he missed you. He would have preferred you kept working for him, of course, even though it would have been awkward at first. He was hurt when you opened up your own agency. But I understood. He did, too, after a while."

"I didn't mean to hurt him."

She nods. "I know."

"I tried to call him once, a year ago," I say, "and again a few months later when I found out about his heart attack, but he never called me back. I thought he hated my guts."

"I tried to call you, more than once. I thought you hated mine."

"What are you talking about?"

"Your girlfriend answered your phone," she says. "Every time. Said you were busy, so I told her to tell you—" Miriam waves her hand. "Doesn't matter." Her face looks broken from the inside, as if with one touch, the outside's gonna fall apart.

"Miriam, I swear I didn't get any messages."

"You mean she didn't tell you," she says. "Never mind. It's okay."

"It's not okay. She's usually really great about giving me messages."

"Uh-huh."

"She is," I say.

Miriam takes a drag from her cigarette and exhales a mushroom of smoke. "You don't have to convince me," she says.

"Why were you calling anyway?"

Miriam looks away. The fountain gurgles.

"What is it?" I ask.

Someone opens one of the French doors and peers outside, squinting into the settling darkness, but then steps inside and shuts the door again.

"I can't have children, Bogey," Miriam says.

"What do you mean?"

"The doctor says my body isn't built for babies."

"That's a terrible thing to say."

"It's the truth." She tosses her cigarette to the ground and crushes it with her shoe. "I'm sorry for all those awful things I said about how you were keeping me from having kids. Apparently it was my body that didn't want them, not you. Or maybe my body was conspiring with you." She smiles, but I don't. "I'm trying to be funny," she says. "Work with me here."

I swallow, and it burns. "I'm sorry, Miriam. I really am. Kids were what you always wanted, more than you wanted anything else."

"Not more than anything else," she says. "Don't say that."

I know it's none of my business, but: "Marco Polo okay with what the doc said?"

"I haven't told him," she says. "I know. Don't judge me."

"I wasn't."

"It's complicated," she says. Miriam always thought everything was complicated when it never was.

The hum of chattering people drifts from the living room windows like it's raining in there but not out here.

"Do you remember the time Chigger ate a whole box of Fig Newtons?" I ask her.

She laughs. I can't remember the last time I said something that made her laugh. "I remember how terrible the house smelled for two days afterward," she says. "I used a whole box of matches to tame the toxicity."

I laugh along with her, a miracle, this, the two of us.

"Would you do it all over again," she asks, "knowing what you know now?"

"What?"

"Us, our marriage?"

"Of course," I say. "No question."

"Really?" She nods and wipes her eyes. "Me, too."

When I get home, Daniela is stretched out on the couch, the fan whirring, making her clothes ripple. Bambi has wedged himself between Daniela and some throw pillows, safe from the wind in the room.

I turn off the fan and touch Daniela's shoulder. "Hey, I'm home."

She sits up, yawns.

"Don't get up," I say. "It's late." I sink into the couch next to her, and Bambi jumps off.

Daniela climbs onto my lap. She is light, nearly weightless, like a fern, something you could step on and flatten if you weren't paying attention. After a minute, Daniela has fallen asleep on me. She doesn't do it very often, but when she does, I have this urge to stay awake and never move.

Suddenly Daniela stirs, opens her eyes, startled to the world. "What happened?"

"Nothing," I say.

She unfolds from my lap, rises to her feet.

"Hey," I say, grabbing her hand to stop her from walking away. "Has Miriam ever called me?"

"Who?"

"My ex-wife, Miriam."

Daniela lets go of my hand and reaches down to scoop up Bambi. She cradles him in her arms, strokes his back. "I don't know," she says.

"You don't know."

"You need to talk to her?" she asks.

"No, it's not that. I mean, I wasn't even aware that she . . . that she . . ." I lean back on the couch. "Forget it. I don't even know why I'm asking." I have to scoot over because the stuffing is coming out and poking me in the back. "So are you gonna tell me about the letter?"

"Hm?"

"This morning," I say. "Who was it from?"

"No one," she says.

"You're telling me that it was no one who wrote you a letter that made you fucking cry?"

She kisses Bambi's face, scratches his ears and then tosses him to the ground. He dashes from the room. Daniela stands in front of me with her hands on her hips. "Yes. No one."

"Seriously? You got nothing right now? Nada?"

"Don't do that, Bogey," she says.

"Don't do what?"

"Don't." She climbs back into my lap. "It was only stupid." She nuzzles her face into my neck.

"Yeah," I say. "Okay. It's okay." And we sit there like that for what feels like forever. It's humid, and she's sticky, and the air is stiff. I wish I hadn't turned off the fan. I wish I'd said nothing. A car honks down the street, *beep-beep-beep*, getting closer. I lay my head on the back of the couch and close my eyes. "I'm gonna write you a book someday," I tell Daniela, I tell the world, I tell that stupid Bambi, wherever he is.

She nods against my chest.

"I really mean it," I say.

Daniela falls asleep again, and I do not dare to move.

THE SNOWSTORM

Seymour shows up in a snowstorm to see her. His chest is like a radiator, and he unfastens the toggle buttons of his wool coat as he stands at a gas station in Oreana, Ohio, just down the street from where Flavia lives now, a street he has never been on before, which he wants to stand on tomorrow, next week, next month, until he can convince her to move away from this rural town and to DC with him.

Seymour did not warn Flavia he was coming, just got into his yellow truck with chains on the tires and clanked through three states that felt like forever. He feels a hum in his chest, this close, but still a few blocks left to go. His hand trembles as he dials the pay phone.

She picks up, *hello*, and he can picture Flavia's sweep of black hair, her chocolate eyes, and the way she puckers her mouth while she waits. He says *it's me*.

"Oh," she says. "It's you."

Snowflakes stutter down all around him.

"I'm glad you called," she says, and he imagines Flavia winding the phone cord like a ring around her finger. "I was going to call you tonight."

"You were?" he says.

"We need to talk."

"Okay." Seymour squints up at the gray sky, which should be so much darker, except for the storm and the streetlamp's fluorescence. "Here I am." He lets snow drop into his eyes.

She says, "I've been thinking a lot about it. I really have. I don't want you to think I haven't, or that I would make some snap decision."

"I know that. I know you."

"But I just don't think we should try again."

Snow sticks to his red beard and wool cap. Wet flakes melt onto his neck. He tucks the phone between his ear and shoulder, tears off his gloves and pushes the toggle buttons back into their nooses, one by one.

"Are you still there?" she asks.

He says he is. He feels wobbly and numb.

"I'm sorry," she says.

"Don't be sorry." The snow has seeped through his right boot, through some crack or crevice Seymour did not know of; his sock is now soggy.

"But I know you were hoping for something else. And I was, too, but."

"Can I see you?"

"Seymour, I don't think that's such a good idea. Last time that happened—"

"I told you—I've changed." He takes hold of the silver umbilical cord connecting the phone to the receiver.

"Seymour—"

"I'm coming over."

"What, tonight? You'll never get a flight. Nothing is landing in this."

"If I come, will you see me?"

He pictures her squinting, as if she were seeing something at a great distance and gauging its danger. He pictures the small gold hoops in her ears, punctuating the sides of her face. A car powers by, spraying Seymour with gray slush.

"I have to be at work early tomorrow morning," she says. "I'm an hour from any major airport. I'm too hard to get to tonight."

"Let me decide that."

She sighs. "Okay, fine. Check the flights yourself. You'll see."

"A snowstorm would never stop me," he says, and when she does not respond, he lets her off the phone. It is better if he faces her. After all these months, he cannot wait any longer, and he fires up the yellow truck, and it chugs him the last few blocks to where he knows he's meant to be.

After Flavia hangs up, she listens to her neighbors through the apartment wall, the clack of a pot or frying pan against their metal sink, and their two voices mingling, weaving strands of their day together. She hears this couple every morning and evening: the shrieks of laughter, the muffled discussions, and then the arguments that rise out of nowhere like a dark flock of crows from a long, shorn field.

Sometimes their voices make her feel less alone. Most of the time they linger like ghosts that never lived there.

Flavia steps into her bedroom and slings her work shoes into the closet's corner. She unzips her houndstooth skirt, and it falls to the floor in a somber heap before she picks it up and clips it to the hanger. The skirt dangles alongside all the other clothes that are too stiff or too itchy but that she wears because they make her feel professional, and stronger. She's sure they're the only reason the students respect her. Even Krystal has finally started showing up every day, her sprinkle of acne and that puff of bruised eye covered by a thick layer of foundation, her pink nail polish chipped, her nails chewed down to the fingers.

Flavia pulls on the baggy pair of sweatpants she never shows in public, not even on a late-night run to the grocery store. The fabric feels soft against her legs and belly.

She doesn't want to think of Seymour's call, which rang in after the storm shuddered its first flakes from her Ohio sky. She opens the refrigerator door and lets the cold ache onto her face and then shuts the door despite the pangs in her stomach. She could more easily ignore those than the storm's now fistfuls of snow. She looks out her window at the world, smothered in white. The snowflakes stick to the window, winter tatting lace against glass.

The doorbell's buzz startles her, and she tiptoes barefoot to the door and stands on the patch of carpet dirtied by her comings and goings. She leans toward the peephole and sees a blank hallway, only her neighbor's door across the way, a door just like Flavia's, so thinly constructed that the frigid air eases in at all hours.

A minute later, the bell buzzes again. Flavia races, but there is no one through the peephole, just an empty hallway with its fluorescent light.

The third buzz, and she doesn't bother looking through the peephole. She jerks open the flimsy door.

"Finally," Seymour says, and he laughs. "I thought you'd never answer."

She takes a step back. Her heart is outrageous in its thumping. "How in the world did you . . . ?" He has grown a thick red beard since the last time they saw each other, when his face was pale and bare against the scorch of Mexican sun.

"You just assumed I was in DC," he says. "I was at a pay phone down the street."

"You drove in this?"

"I wanted to surprise you."

"Seymour, I swear, you can't just show up like this."

"But I asked this time."

She shakes her head and laughs then, realizing how silly this is: Seymour all the way from DC, standing outside her front door—his mess of shaggy red hair, the silver stud in his ear, the way he shifts from side to side when trying to stand still. And here she is, not letting him in after weeks of wanting to. Flavia reaches out her hand to him. "Come in."

"Don't I get a hug?"

"Oh, Seymour, of course you do," and she puts her arms around him. He smells, as he always did, of soil and rain. Through his thick coat she can feel his warmth. She shudders, and she forces herself to let go, the way she did before, the way she knows she must again.

Flavia is making him tea. Seymour watches her pulling the boxes from the cupboards and lifting out the tiny bags and dunking them into the hiss of hot water. He is remembering her in his studio apartment in Cincinnati, how she made him instant coffee every morning—it was all either of them could afford as students. Sometimes, when she had an extra few dollars, she bought tamarind candy at the dimly lit Mexican grocery in his neighborhood. She'd cut the candy into little sweet and sour pieces and serve them on yellow paper napkins, and it felt like a party with her chattering, sitting beside him wearing one of his oversized T-shirts. He loved the dimple in her left cheek, her slight overbite, her thick eyebrows, the way she smelled like cinnamon.

Now, she is making small talk—*how's work with the congressman,* she is asking, and *are you able to ride your bike in DC*—and he is answering he loves his work, telling her yes, he bikes to the office, sometimes he's so sweaty when he gets there he has to wash up in the men's room and people look at him funny as he takes wads of paper towels and wipes off his back. This makes her laugh, and he feels relieved to see her smile. She's seemed so serious over email and on the phone the last two months, ever since he contacted her after so long a silence, and now all he wants is to look at her for the rest of his life.

He knows she is nervous because she does not stop stirring and stirring, hitting the spoon against the porcelain.

"Please come sit down with me," he says, and she picks up both cups and takes slow steps toward him, keeping her gaze on the levels of hot water that swishes back and forth toward the tops of the cups, nearly flowing over.

It was only two weeks ago, the day after Christmas when she was back home in Akron, that Flavia told her mother that Seymour had contacted her in early December.

Her mother was cooking, slicing onions on a chopping board, wiping her eyes with her sleeve. "What did he want this time?"

Flavia shrugged. "Just to talk."

"So is that what you're doing?"

"It's different than before. It's good. It really is. We've been talking about what happened."

"*You* have, or *he* has?"

"Both, Mami. He's really trying."

"Is this because you're lonely?"

Flavia thought of the one man she'd dated in the last year—the only male teacher in the county school. He wore jeans belted with a big brass buckle, and his belly hung slightly over his waistband. He had a chipped front tooth, and he hummed more than spoke. When he did speak, it was softly, and he never interrupted her, had no big opinions, and Flavia had to prod him to make even the slightest decision—which of two restaurants to go to, what carton of ice cream to buy—until she could stand it no longer. Now, he avoided her in the lunchroom and teacher's lounge.

"I just miss Seymour sometimes."

"Come home. Your *papi* will find you a job."

"You're not listening."

"What do you want from me, Flavia?"

"I just want you to be open."

"You can't ask me that," her mother said. "Not again."

"But I am."

Her mother set down the knife and wiped her hands on the apron front. "It's your life, *querida*. But do me a favor."

"What's that?"

"Don't tell your *papi*." Her mother dropped the onions into the waiting pan. "This would kill him."

They've finished the tea, and the cups sit cold and empty on the floor. Seymour remembers the last argument they had, after he'd surprised her in Mexico, just before he left to catch his plane back to the States. Flavia had flinched when he raised his voice, again. He hadn't meant to, again. He wanted her to come back with him, to give up the teaching job, leave behind the little adobe house, the hard twin bed, the bowl of wet and green *nopales*, the clay jar of *jocoque* kept chilled in ice. A straw hat let the sun trickle onto her face and olive skin when she said no, but it had seemed more noble then, to give him up for the scrawny yet spirited children in torn T-shirts.

Now, Flavia is saying, "I'm scared nothing has changed."

"You're scared of me?" He feels sick to his stomach.

She lifts her shoulders, lets them fall. "I'm scared of who I was with you."

He covers her hand with his. "You were happy." What he means is no one else will ever make her happy. He is absolutely sure of that.

She removes her hand from beneath his and shakes her head. "I got lost."

"I know I didn't listen, but I am now. And if you still don't want to move to DC—"

"It was never about DC."

"I'll move here. Or we'll pick a place. Just tell me what you want."

"We'd still be the same people."

"I hardly drink anymore," he says. He is sweating with chills now, remembering the bruise on her arm she showed him once, after he had sobered up. The bruise wrapped like a black snake around the place he had clutched to keep her from leaving.

She gives him her hand again now, but her face crumples when she says, "The last thing I want is to hurt you."

Seymour has his mother's eyes, large and longing. Flavia met her the only time Seymour ever brought Flavia home to rural Missouri. Flavia sank next to Seymour on the plaid couch as his parents flipped from *Wheel of Fortune* to *Andy Griffith* reruns. She slept in Seymour's old bedroom in the back of the farmhouse, but she could still hear his father yelling late at night when he'd had too much to drink. Seymour crept into her room later, when he whispered that he was sure his father would not hear, would be passed out on the couch. She kept Seymour warm, her body thick to his slimness. When they left after two days—a day earlier than planned—Seymour's mother stood on the porch, one bone-thin hand holding on to the railing, the other hand waving goodbye. His mother looked straight into the sun as if she did not notice it anymore. His father had not emerged from the barn, not that morning for their cold-cereal breakfast and not even when Seymour's mother had called for him as Flavia and Seymour carried their bags to the truck. They'd heard the clanking of machinery from the half-open, splintery door. The sounds drifted to them and then faded as if in a swallowing fog.

Seymour lies on his back on Flavia's lumpy couch. The living room is as dark as his worry. Flavia has left her bedroom door open, and she is coughing. He remembers the nights her allergies kept her awake throughout spring and summer. Even in the city, pollen and ragweed loitered through his open windows.

This apartment is nothing like Flavia. It is a place drained of color and comedy. He wants to give that back to her. He is sure he can.

The apartment bleeds with quiet. All evening, he was trying to make his voice, usually commanding and booming, soft. He knows she can hear him if he barely says it, so he does. "Can you hold me?" He can't think of what else to ask.

Seymour consumes the space in her bedroom doorway.

Flavia says, "It's too much."

"Doesn't that tell you what we feel isn't going away?"

When Flavia doesn't answer, Seymour trudges back to the couch. She listens for the rattling of his breathing.

Here's what Flavia remembers: their voices echoing against metal pipes that crossed his kitchen ceiling, the peppermint plant she potted that failed to grow on his Cincinnati windowsill.

Here's what Seymour remembers: the warmth of her feet, how slowly she ate avocado, the cards she made him cut from magazines and construction paper, the tortillas she rolled with potato and then fried in his one wide pan.

She remembers the label sweating off his beer bottle, the night they argued so hard she lost her voice for three days.

He remembers the only thing she said as they drove from his farm in Missouri: "I'm so sorry."

She remembers all the times, so many now, he said, "I'm so sorry."

He remembers salsa jars she washed and kept on shelves and tables, jars filled with clumps of dandelions, their stems browning in the water.

She remembers the scraggly dog they found and nearly kept, the pregnancy test and the cramping three days later, the weight she gained, the weight she lost.

He remembers the brisk and windy day, not long after the cramping, when she insisted he teach her how to change a tire, how she wouldn't let him help her turn the wrench, how she cried when the new tire was on, when it was over.

She remembers the passenger door of his yellow truck that never shut unless you slammed it; the enchiladas he burned, made from her mother's recipe to try and cheer her up; how he begged her old and happy self to come back to him.

He remembers the nightmares she shook him from, saying, "Come back to me."

She remembers the blue-beaded necklace he gave her for Christmas, the water-pearl ring for her birthday, the salsa lessons he took even though he could not afford them.

He remembers the black galoshes and orange plastic poncho she wore when she walked along the creek bed with him, looking for rocks, no matter how hard it rained.

She remembers Sunday nights when he made grilled cheese sandwiches cut into quarters for dinner as if they were kids, and how they played bingo using her grandmother's old game cards with the gold sombrero, the mermaid *sirena* and the red-horned *diablito*.

He, the white skies of winter when he'd look up and wonder where she was.

She, the blue skies woven with jet streams, from airplanes going somewhere, away.

He, the sound of her footsteps, listening for them.

She, the twelve steps to his apartment, how she counted them each time except the last.

He, the Spanish words she taught him: *beso, luz, vida*—kiss, light, life.

She, the Spanish words she should have taught him: *hambre, dolor, extrañar*—hunger, pain, and the verb for what you feel when you've lost something you wished you still possessed.

Maybe no one will ever love her the way he does.

Flavia slips from her bed.

"Scoot over," she says, and once she is settled beside him, "This isn't a yes."

"I'll take whatever it is."

Flavia lets the snow become a sort of white amnesia. Already she is drifting away.

He watches her sleeping, feels her leg curled over his. One hand is balled into a fist, and he wonders if that's how she always sleeps now, if this is the new Flavia, or if it's because of him.

The only way to prove he's changed is to let her go—the one thing he said he'd never do. Is that what it will take?

As the sky turns milky with morning, Flavia hears the town's snow-plow rumble its way down her street and knows the storm has not stopped time, has not buried them together for another day. Isn't that what she really wanted?

Ohio natives always handle their snow, and in rural counties, people plod on. She can picture the plow heaving blank and dazzling white to the side, baring dirty and pocked pavement below. Her students will know to show up, some of them smoking a last cigarette outside the school's doors. The girls will be wearing thick black eyeliner, tight turtleneck sweaters, pretending not to notice or care about the boys jostling and joking in the crowded parking lot. The girls won't be wearing coats. Their shoulders will be hunched.

Flavia moves to lift herself off the couch, and Seymour puts his arm around her waist to stop her. "Don't go," he says.

"You have to," she says.

"Please, Flavia." But she is already rising into the gray light of the apartment and closing her bedroom door.

After she has showered and dressed, Flavia re-emerges, crossing into the living room where the couch waits, empty. She half expected to see Seymour lying there still, arm flung over his head, but instead the sheets and blanket are folded in a stack, and his clothes, which had lingered on a chair, have disappeared. He's done exactly what she asked him to, and the relief she expects to feel in floods instead just gives a trickle.

Flavia pulls on some boots and tugs on her coat. Her car will be completely and utterly buried, so she rummages in her closet for the bigger snow scraper. But once outside, instead of a mound of snow, she finds her hatchback glittering blue, every bit of white powder carefully brushed away from it. The car gleams in the weak morning sun, and Flavia stares at it for a few moments before she forces herself into the car and slams the door. She does not turn on the engine.

She thinks of Krystal, who will want to eat lunch—always just a bag of corn chips and a half-pint carton of chocolate milk—in the safety of Flavia's empty classroom while Flavia grades papers. Flavia wonders where she can get tamarind candy, a treat she used to buy when she felt unsteady. Its taste, sugary but kicked with tang, clung to her mouth for hours. She imagines cutting the candy into little pieces—the only way to make a thing tolerable—and placing them on paper napkins. She imagines handing them to Krystal, who will nod and accept what Flavia has to offer, though it will be a thing of opposites, sweet with spice, like fickleness and constancy, nostalgia and regret.

Flavia imagines kissing Seymour, his mouth tangy and sweet, and she feels a familiar wobbly feeling, so she twists the key in the ignition and chugs on the engine. Flavia clutches the steering wheel, even though the car remains parked, until the engine's warm and steady rumble is enough to go on.

TRYING TO GROW

As soon as Nathaniel's boss green-lighted the training, Nathaniel started counting down the four weeks until Claims College. In preparation, he drove to a pharmacy in a town fifteen miles outside of Columbus, Ohio, paid cash for a six-count box of condoms—surely enough—and locked it in the station wagon's glove box. And he started growing a mustache. The first time Nathaniel had ever grown one was two decades ago, when he was a senior in high school and on top of the world.

"What's *that*?" Maggie said, pointing with a spatula at the fuzz on his upper lip two nights later. Nathaniel's wife had just shoveled the snowy driveway, so she was wearing her polka-dotted fleece pants and rubber winter boots and one of his Ohio Dominion sweatshirts with a bleach stain across the front.

Nathaniel cocked his head to the side, puffed out his chest, and flashed her a smile. "You like it?"

"The last time you grew one of those you were going through some pre-midlife crisis. You started shopping for a muscle car," she said. "As if that were gonna happen."

"Can't a man just look at a car?" He still sometimes wished he'd had the guts to slap down a credit card and buy that yellow Corvette, but Maggie would have taken a baseball bat to it. Or him. "I didn't buy anything, remember?"

"Because I called *your mother.*"

"I'm keeping the mustache," Nathaniel said.

Maggie had her back to him now as she cooked at the stove. "Can the mustache take out the garbage? Or is it too busy trying to grow?"

Claims College, held in Connecticut, was where everyone at SafeNation Insurance went to get trained. It was revered as one of the top insurance training programs in the country, and to insiders, it was celebrated as the biggest week of booty calls, affairs, and hookups. Nathaniel had once heard a coworker say if you didn't get laid at Claims College, then you were either too drunk or too dead.

Nathaniel had been to Claims College twice. The first time was when he'd started at the insurance agency ten years ago, back when he was twenty-eight and he and Maggie were newlyweds. He'd spent the entire week either in training sessions or, between sessions, whispering *I love you* and *I miss you* to Maggie by phone, hoping that the more he said it the longer he could fend off his fading feelings. The second time was five years ago, and he had thought briefly of the possibility of getting his nerve up for just one little hookup. He could do that, right? Isn't this what men did all the time? It didn't have to become an issue. After all, that was during the eighteen months that Maggie had stopped having sex with him, just after the twins were born, a contrast to the sex duties and sex calendar (as he had thought of them) that Maggie had made him keep when trying to conceive a second child. But right before that training, Nathaniel got the flu and spent the week clutching his stomach and trying not to inhale the smell of food. It had occurred to him this might be some sort of punishment for having impure thoughts, but his rational side noted that Maggie had gotten sick, too, just not as badly. He didn't let himself think she might need punishment, too.

Now, Nathaniel had just gotten a promotion—the biggest promotion of his career. He was different now, wasn't he? More than the money, he liked the effect on his status at work: the bigger, private office and the way the higher-ups noticed him and stopped to ask how he was doing instead of just nodding at him as he passed them in the hall, or worse, ignoring him. He was now handling larger injury claims, general liability stuff: the broken backs from tripping over broken sidewalks, the drownings in hotel pools. They didn't seem like a big deal to Nathaniel, just more of the same, only with larger claims.

Maggie had asked him once how he handled hearing about depressing incidents all day long.

"I'm helping people," he said. "Someone's got to."

"But what about when you don't want to give them as much as they want for their losses?" she said.

"No one gets everything they want," he said. "That's life."

Sometimes he thought about Becky, his one and only high school girlfriend. They'd been on the debate team together their senior year, but she'd always been smarter, able to generate arguments out of air while Nathaniel had needed much more preparation and research. Back then he had stammered when nervous, and under bright lights, this stammering, he knew, resembled failure and ineptitude. But Becky had never made him feel like he was doing anything but winning.

Becky had brown curly hair, which she'd worn in a puff of a ponytail. She had freckles and red-framed glasses with thick lenses. Once, when they'd been making out on the corduroy couch in her parents' den long after her parents had gone to sleep, she admitted to Nathaniel she could barely see him without her glasses, unless he was up close. He pictured himself fuzzying in and out of her view, and he pulled back and leaned in, pulled back and leaned in, teasing her, "Do you see me now, or now? How about now?"

"Stop it," she'd said and pulled him in. "You're not my Mister Wonderful unless you're right here in front of me."

That's when he knew he would love Becky forever, even if she broke up with him. Which, on the first day of that summer twenty years ago, she promptly did.

The morning he was to leave for Claims College, Nathaniel's mustache was thick and what Maggie would have called "woolly" had she been commenting on his mustache, which she had stopped doing.

"Just don't kiss me with that thing" was all she said in reference to it. "Let me know when it's over."

Maggie had agreed to take him to the airport after she dropped off the kids at school. "Come on!" she yelled up the stairs. Her voice boomed all the way into the kitchen, where Nathaniel was sipping his cup of decaf. Sometimes Nathaniel thought Maggie would make a great football coach. This thought also scared him.

"Your daddy needs to be on time to make his flight!" she shouted. "Let's hustle, hustle, hustle!" Maggie banged the kitchen door open and stuck her head in. "Ready? Kids are in the van."

"I'll be right there." Nathaniel had forgotten to empty the glove box in the station wagon. "Gotta get something out of my car."

"Better get a move on it, or this bus is leaving."

After he'd retrieved the box and stuffed it into his carry-on, he strode to the van and pulled open the passenger side. His nine-year-old son was sitting in the seat.

"Sorry," Maggie said. "He asked. I said yes. Just hop in the back with the girls."

With his carry-on hugged tight against his chest, Nathaniel sat squished between two little braided girls in their boosters on the middle bench seat because their dolls, they told him, were asleep in the very back.

"Buckle up," his son said, and Nathaniel did.

"Yo! Nat!" It was Octavio from Iowa City. He was the only person who ever called Nathaniel "Nat." Octavio was waving his arms wildly from the bar.

Nathaniel pushed by the other claims reps who were all crowded into Forevers, the hotel bar.

They thumped each other on the back. Nathaniel almost coughed because Octavio had an arm as strong and hard as a two-by-four.

"How's it goin', man?" Octavio said.

"It's great," Nathaniel said. "Awesome to be here."

"You're tellin' me, man. This place is hoppin'. I've been nursin' this beer for the last half hour, trying not to get wasted the first night. Boss is here." He shoved an elbow into Nathaniel. "Gotta keep it clean, know what I mean?"

Nathaniel surveyed the throng of people, looking for the who's who in the SafeNation world, but mostly he was scanning for single ladies.

"You hear Tammy got that crazy case out of L.A.?" Octavio said. He unbuttoned his cuffs and rolled up his shirtsleeves. "Did a fine-ass job on it, too. Got that Employee of the Year award and everything. Man, this company is all about Tammy now. She is smokin'." He leaned in closer to Nathaniel, who still had on his suit jacket. "And I can tell you right now success looks sweet on that woman."

Nathaniel remembered the annual conference two years ago when Tammy and Octavio had spent two days in a row ordering room service. He kept calling Octavio every time he didn't show for a meeting.

Nathaniel asked Octavio, "Are you all still . . . ?"

"Nah, man. I'm done with all that," Octavio said. "Me and Sins, we made it official." Sindee was his on-and-off girlfriend and had been the seven years since Nathaniel had known him. Octavio had once shown Nathaniel pictures of Sindee from a trip they'd taken to Vegas. She was buxom and full-lipped and wore heavy makeup and eyeshadow that made her look like a raccoon.

"Congratulations," Nathaniel said as he tried unsuccessfully to signal the bartender. "When'd you get married?"

"Last summer, man. Sindee's preggers already. Due in three months."

"That's great."

"I'm settlin' down, my friend," Octavio said. "Gonna be a quiet week for me here. What about you? Wife still got you by the balls?"

Nathaniel coughed, and Octavio laughed and slapped him on the back.

"I'm just messin' with you, buddy. I know you got the whole Beaver Cleaver family thing goin' on. That's cool. But if you ever want some wrinkle in that starched shirt of yours . . ." He raised an eyebrow and looked around and said, "This is it, man. Take it or leave it, but don't say you weren't given the gift."

Nathaniel wanted the gift, he just wasn't sure he wanted to tell Octavio about it. He'd rather brag about it later than have to confess to anyone (especially Octavio) that he hadn't gotten any action. Octavio—with his gelled hair, his big gold Iowa State school ring, the stud in his ear—looked like action without even doing anything.

Nathaniel tried to puff himself up before dinner that night, standing in front of the bathroom mirror with his suit and tie on, checking his hair—he had combed it in a way that really covered up the places it was thinning. He leaned close to the mirror to inspect his teeth. He'd been using white strips for the last two weeks, and they'd mostly done their job and bleached off the coffee stains. He stepped back and cocked his head to the side, considering: did he look too uptight? He tore off the jacket, loosened the tie, and fluffed his hair just a bit. He wanted to look as if he'd been having a good time, and as if he meant it.

At the entrance to the hotel ballroom, Nathaniel examined the crowd and found Octavio, who was sitting at a table and laughing with his head thrown back, on either side of him a woman. On his left was Tammy with a plunging neckline, bright pink lipstick, and hair so over-sprayed it didn't move as she shook with laughter; on Octavio's right was a young woman with straight, mousy brown hair that was thinning at the ends, her suit jacket buttoned all the way and looking a little too tight, revealing nothing but her flat chest. She wasn't laughing. She was glancing around the ballroom, as if someone were following her.

"Nat, my man." Octavio stood and shook Nathaniel's hand as if he hadn't just seen him two hours earlier. He motioned to Tammy. "You remember Miss Tammy? Los Angeles now but used to be Charlotte, North Carolina."

"Of course." Nathaniel extended a hand. "Looking beautiful, as always."

"She is, she is," Octavio chimed in.

"Oh, thank you so much." Tammy fanned her face. "You all are much too kind."

"And this is Tammy's niece, uh . . ." Octavio was motioning to the young woman. "Tammy's niece, uh . . ."

"It's Bridget." She glared at Octavio. "Charlotte, North Carolina."

Octavio ignored the glare. "Bridge is a newbie," he said to Nathaniel. "Just started on auto claims a few months ago. She might be able to, you know," he winked at Nathaniel, "use some mentoring."

"Sure," Nathaniel said. He hoped his face was not turning the red that he felt roasting his neck. He shook her hand. Her grip was limp and lifeless. "I'm, um, Nat. Columbus, Ohio."

Bridget nodded and slumped back against her seat and pulled out her phone. Octavio and Tammy turned to each other once more, their bodies leaning toward one another and forming a V like a tent for two.

Nathaniel sat down beside Bridget. "So, how do you like SafeNation?"

"It's fine."

"Octavio said you're in auto?"

"Yep." She was scrolling through something on her phone.

"That's the best place to start," Nathaniel said. "Auto."

"Isn't that where everyone starts?"

"Yes, but, I'm just saying it's good. I started there a long time ago, worked my way up."

"Good for you."

"So," he said, "have you checked out the new SafeNation app?"

"Nope."

"It's pretty impressive." He cleared his throat. "I hear texting is the rage these days," he said.

She looked up. "Did you just say 'the rage'?"

He brightened. "I did. So you like texting?"

Head back down. "Yep."

Nathaniel drummed his fingers on the table and reached for a glass of iced tea. Beads of water dripped down the sides of the glass. "Texting your boyfriend?" he finally asked.

She narrowed her eyes. "Why?"

Sweat was forming on his back and neck. "Just curious. You, um, seem like a nice girl who might have a boyfriend."

"Please tell me you're not hitting on me. You're like a billion years older than I am."

Nathaniel opened his mouth to respond and then thought better of it and gulped down the entire glass of tea.

The next night, Nathaniel was exhausted from the first day of training—on evaluating claims and the most complex and multiple losses—but he'd agreed to meet Octavio for a drink after dinner. Maggie had left him a voicemail asking him to call back as soon as he could, but he didn't feel like talking.

The Forevers dance floor was a pool of wet bodies all shoved together and bouncing up and down to the same thump-thump-thump beat. Nathaniel spotted Octavio right away grooving on the dance floor: he and Tammy had their arms raised in the air, and Tammy was dancing with her back and butt smashed against Octavio's chest and abdomen. He didn't look very newlywedded.

Nathaniel studied the entire room, hoping to find some woman waiting to be talked to. Instead, Bridget was across the way, sitting at the bar, texting. He nudged his way past the people pressed against the bar and signaled the bartender, who frowned but came over. Bridget glanced up and gave a brief wave at Nathaniel without smiling and then returned to texting. After he got his drink, Nathaniel pushed his way over to her. He had to shout to be heard. "You're not dancing?"

She shook her head. "I'm waiting for Aunt Tammy," she shouted back. "I'm the designated driver."

"You're not staying here at the hotel?"

"What'd you say?" She plugged one ear and leaned in.

"You're not staying at the hotel?" he shouted again.

"Oh, I meant I'm supposed to make sure she doesn't sleep with him." She pointed to Octavio, whose eyes were now closed and whose arms were draped around Tammy's waist. "At least that was her official request."

"No offense," Nathaniel said, "but you don't seem like you're doing a very good job."

She shrugged. "People say things all the time they don't really mean." Bridget went back to texting and then set her phone on top of the bar. "Hey, Nat," she shouted, "I'm sorry for giving you a hard time the other night. Octavio told me you're happily married and totally harmless."

"He said that?"

"Said you were the opposite of a ladies' man."

"Well, I wouldn't exactly say—"

"Let's start over," she shouted. She extended her hand. "I'm Bridget."

Nathaniel shook it. Her grip was stronger. "Wanna dance, Bridget?"

"I'm seriously awful at dancing," she said.

"I am, too, but I have a feeling no one is looking at us."

She scanned the room. "Okay." She lifted her pointer finger. "One dance."

And that's how Nathaniel ended up dancing with a twenty-something for the first time since he'd danced with Maggie at their wedding. He and Bridget didn't press up against each other. The distance between them would have been much greater had it not been for drunk insurance agents swaying into them and pushing them only a foot apart. Nathaniel didn't care that Bridget didn't close her eyes, that she spent the entire song glancing around to make sure no one was watching. He didn't care that she didn't stamp her feet in time with the beat, that she kept her arms pinned to her sides. He snapped his fingers in the air and swayed, and for a few moments, he even closed his eyes.

Once they walked out of Forevers, they didn't have to shout anymore. The thump-thump-thump faded as they strolled away and down the hotel hall toward the lobby. Bridget was carrying her heels in one hand. "I can't believe she left the bar without me."

"You mean that she left with Octavio."

Bridget shook her head. "I'm out there dancing for just a few songs—"

"It was more than a few."

"—and she sneaks out."

"She didn't have to sneak." Nathaniel was laughing. "You were pretty into it, especially that last set." He imitated her twirling with her arms in the air. "Admit it. You had a good time."

She rolled her eyes. "Fine." They ambled through the lobby toward the elevator. "You think they're in Octavio's room, right?" she asked.

"I thought he was rooming with his boss."

"Dang it. I knew I should have gotten my own room."

"You're with Tammy?"

She pointed to one of the couches in the lobby. "Think they'd mind if I curled up on one of those?"

"You don't have to do that," Nathaniel said. He was trying to keep his voice from sounding high and uncertain. "Stay with me."

"Seriously?"

"Sure. I have two doubles."

"Your wife wouldn't object?"

"I'm not asking," Nathaniel said. He pressed the up button for the elevator.

"Are you sure this isn't some ploy to get in my pants?"

Nathaniel laughed and held his arms straight in front and twisted them so she could view both sides. "See? No tricks up the sleeves."

"I *am* exhausted," Bridget said. The elevator doors opened. "And I don't want to see Octavio naked."

Nathaniel punched the button for the sixth floor. "It's settled then."

When Nathaniel emerged from the bathroom, Bridget's black suit jacket and pants and her thin white blouse were draped over a chair, and Bridget was already asleep in the other bed, making little snoring sounds. He was disappointed—he was hoping against hope that something might still happen, but he was also relieved since the lights were on. He didn't want Bridget to see him without his shirt and pants, to see his untoned arms and skinny legs, his bit of a beer belly (which actually wasn't big from beer but from too much candy, which Maggie kept all around the house for the kids). If Bridget saw him half naked, she might really be convinced he was too old. He threw the robe off and quickly slipped under the covers. He glanced over at Bridget to make sure she hadn't stirred—he was hoping she might and also not hoping—but she lay still, and he switched off the light.

Bridget was prettier than he first thought. And he'd had a good time dancing, probably the best time he'd had in years. He'd felt lighter on that wooden floor, smashed against everyone else, and for a moment, as he swayed to the rhythms, he'd forgotten about the training and Octavio and Tammy, and Maggie back at home.

Maggie. He reached for the phone on the nightstand to check his texts. There was only one from her, at 11:02 p.m.: *Call me as soon as you get this*.

He turned off the ringer and put the phone facedown on his nightstand.

Nathaniel jolted up when the hotel phone shrilled through the room. For a moment he was disoriented, and then he realized where he was and that it was morning. He grabbed the phone.

"Why didn't you call me back last night?"

The light spilled in through the break between the curtains, and Bridget's bed was empty, her clothes gone from the chair. "It was a late night," he said. He lay back and put a hand on his chest to calm his thwacking heartbeat.

"I bet it was," Maggie said. "Well, for your information, your mom's in the hospital. She fell and broke a hip, but they think she also has a concussion."

"What? When?"

"Last night, around 7:30. At least that's when I got the call. Thank God some neighbor came by to drop off something and could hear the TV on really loud. The neighbor thought it was strange when no one came to the door, so she, well, broke in."

"Oh my god. What should I do?"

Maggie gave an exasperated sigh. "I don't know, Nathaniel. Go get yourself another beer?"

"I just meant—should I come home?"

"I knew what you meant," she said. "It was a rough night, and I'm running on fumes. The kids and I were in the ER with Nana until 2:30 this morning when the hospital finally had a room for her. I'm headed back to see her after I take the kids to school and get some of her things for her at her house. Why don't I call you back when I know how serious her concussion is."

"Okay," he said. "I'll wait."

"But you have to answer your phone."

"Of course," Nathaniel said. And in that moment, he meant it.

◆◆◆

Nathaniel got a text from Maggie as he was walking into Forevers for lunch: *Call me.*

He texted back: *In training. Will call soon.*

Nathaniel searched the room for Bridget: she was seated with Tammy and Octavio at a four-top. Bridget smiled and waved when she saw him. Had she been watching for him?

"Nat, my man," said Octavio in a booming voice, and he thumped Nathaniel on the back. "Take a seat."

"We were just plotting our evening," Tammy said. "We're gonna ditch the BBQ dinner and head off to a Mexican place down the street."

"Sounds good," Nathaniel said. "Everyone going?"

Bridget nodded.

"Then I'm in," he said.

"My man Nat had some pretty good dance moves last night, am I right?"

"But you didn't tell me he was a liar," Bridget said.

Nathaniel tensed. Bridget crossed her arms.

"Nat?" Octavio was looking from Bridget to Nathaniel and back to Bridget. "A liar?"

"He said he couldn't dance," Bridget said. "So I got up and made a total fool of myself thinking we'd be fools together."

Nathaniel felt the air return to his lungs. He exhaled a nervous laugh. "Well I assure you I felt very foolish."

"We saw you two kickin' it out on that dance floor," Octavio said. "Me and Tammy, we were impressed. You outlasted us."

"Well, I only stayed because Nat made it fun." Bridget smiled again, and Nathaniel felt like he was eighteen.

Nathaniel called Maggie after lunch.

"Can't you step out of training for one minute to make a call about your injured mother? They let you out to pee, don't they? Isn't she more important than pee?"

"It was at a critical point," Nathaniel said.

"Whatever," Maggie said. "She's stabilized now, and the doctor thinks she has a mild concussion, but he wants to keep an eye on her, maybe run a few tests this afternoon."

"That's great news."

"But I think something's seriously wrong."

"I thought you said—"

"She keeps calling me Becky. Wasn't that your high school girlfriend?"

"I don't know," Nathaniel said. His mother was the only person he ever told that Becky was the love of his life. But that was years ago. "I mean, I guess, yeah, her name was Becky."

"It's weird. And it's scaring the bejeezus out of me."

"But you said the doctor thinks—

"I told you what the doc thinks, and now I'm telling you what I think."

"Well I hope you're wrong."

"I'm sure you do," Maggie said. "Your mother keeps asking when you're coming home. What do you want me to tell her?"

"Friday. My flight gets in—"

"So you're not coming home early?" Maggie asked.

It sounded like a question, but it felt like a trap. "I'm just going by what the doctor said."

"I gotta go, Nathaniel. I have a family to hold together."

Nathaniel turned off his phone for the rest of the afternoon, telling himself he was saving the batteries. Just before dinner he turned it back on but then left it on the nightstand as he walked out the door.

The Mexican restaurant was decorated with colorful piñatas, a lit-up cactus in the corner, and sequined sombreros hanging from the walls. Octavio bought everyone a round of margaritas and held up his for a toast: "To old friends and new friends!" They clinked their glasses.

"And to surprises," Bridget added, and they all clinked again.

After dinner they walked back to the hotel, Tammy and Octavio in front, her arm linked through his.

"So, what surprises?" Nathaniel asked Bridget.

"Huh?"

"Your toast. What surprises?"

"Oh, that. It's just, I didn't expect to enjoy this training at all, and I really am. It's been a fun week so far."

"Good," Nathaniel said. "I think so, too." He watched her from the corner of his eye. "I've been especially glad I met you."

"Me, too," Bridget said.

He pointed to Octavio and Tammy. "What do you think will happen to them, afterward?"

Bridget shrugged. "Aunt Tammy will go back to her wild self in L.A. Octavio will have a baby in a few months. You know what they say: what happens at Claims College . . ."

Nathaniel raised his eyebrows. "So you approve?"

"The one thing I've learned for sure in the insurance world is that life changes in less than a minute, so grab what you can."

After the foursome had a cocktail at Forevers, and after Bridget and Tammy went to the ladies' room together for nearly fifteen minutes, Bridget ended up in Nathaniel's room again. "Thanks," she told him, sitting on the edge of the bed and removing her suit jacket. "I said no until she resorted to begging. My mother warned me not to room with her, so I consider it my fault for not listening. Thanks for picking up the pieces. Again."

"No problem at all."

"She said he'd be out of there in a few hours."

"It's really okay."

"I'm a little buzzed, so I'm gonna lie down," Bridget said. "Just pretend I'm not here."

"Why would I do that?"

"So you can have some time to think."

"I don't want to think. I want to talk to you," he said. "Well, what I mean is—"

Bridget put her hand up. "It's okay." She was laughing. "I get it. But you really mean that? I would think with a wife and three kids, you'd be dying for some time to just ruminate."

"Nope." He lay back on his pillows, put his hands behind his head. "This is perfect."

"Good." She kicked off her shoes and lay back against her pillows. "Nat, do you think we'll ever see each other again, after this?"

He wasn't sure what she was asking. He felt as he often did with Maggie, like he could screw up without even knowing there was a trial in the question, a verdict in his answer. "I don't know," he said. "Do you?"

"Is there an extra blanket in here? I think I might need it."

She wasn't even under the covers, but he got up off the bed anyway and found a ragged brown blanket in the closet.

"Here." He held it out to her.

Bridget took it. "Wait," she said. "Sit down." She patted the space beside her on the bed. "I have a question."

"Sure," he said, obeying. "What's up?" His hands were shaking, so he sat on them.

"It's not an insurance question, although Octavio tells me you're the best in the business. Says you're now top dog in your office or something like that."

Nathaniel laughed. "Octavio's exaggerating."

"Is he?"

"Well, I mean," Nathaniel was nodding now, "I guess I'm one of the top dogs." Which wasn't exactly true, but he liked how it felt. He liked the admiration in Bridget's eyes.

"That's cool," Bridget said. "You should be proud of that, you know what I mean?"

"Sure," he said. "So was that the question?"

"Octavio can't say enough good things about you. Calls you his best bro." She was gazing down at the bedspread between them, fidgeting with the gaudy red flowers against an ugly brown. "Says how smart you are. Really looks up to you."

"You've been talking to Octavio about me?"

"And I didn't really think smart was one of the things I liked, I mean, I tend to like the bad boys, you know?"

"Sure," he said. "Bad boys. Yeah."

"But I'm beginning to think bad boys aren't so good for me." She smoothed the bedspread with her hand, her swipes touching his leg briefly. "Maybe the smart and nerdy ones are the ones I should be going for, you know?"

"Is that the question?" he asked.

"What do you think about me, Nat?"

"What?"

"Tammy says she thinks you like me. Do you?" She stopped smoothing out the bedspread. Her hand lingered against the side of his leg, making it tingle.

"Of course."

"I don't mean as a friend. I mean, you know, like like."

"She said that?" he asked.

"Is she right? I know I gave you a hard time before about hitting on me, and I'm not accusing you. You've been so sweet, a perfect gentleman."

"But?"

"But what?" Bridget asked.

"Is that the question?" He hoped his leg wasn't trembling because he'd lost most of the feeling in it now.

Bridget rolled her eyes. "You and the question. Sure, yes, that's the question."

"What's the question again?" he asked.

"Is Tammy right—that you're into me?"

Nathaniel felt as he often did with Maggie's questions, innocent and guilty, not sure which he was supposed to be. "Do you want Tammy to be right?"

She tilted her head. "A little."

"Oh," he said, disappointed. His whole lot in life felt like just a little.

"Nat." She jabbed him in the shoulder. "Stop looking like someone died. A little's good."

"It is?"

"Are you and your mustache gonna kiss me or what?"

When he did, he closed his eyes, and he imagined a girl with puffy hair and red-framed glasses. He touched Bridget's face and scooted closer.

"That's right," she whispered. "Come to mama."

His eyes flew open, but Bridget's were now closed. He kissed her again and put his jittery hands on her arms.

"Oh, you're a bad boy, aren't you," she whispered. "I like it when bad boys touch me. How bad are you, Nat?"

He swallowed. "Bad," he croaked out. "So bad."

"That's what I thought. And what do bad boys say to bad girls?"

"I'm bad," he said. He leaned in to kiss her again.

She put her hands on his chest and gently pushed him away from her. "No, I wanna hear you say some *bad* things to me." She kissed him on the mouth and then stopped and waited.

"You're a bad girl, Bridget." He kissed her neck.

"Make it badder," she whispered in his ear.

"You're a very bad girl, Bridget." He pushed her blouse from her shoulder.

"Seriously?" she said, pulling back. "That's the best you can come up with? C'mon, Nat. This isn't PBS. Make it hot."

He was sweating now. "You're making me hot," he said in his deepest voice and started undoing the buttons down the front of her blouse. "Real hot."

"That's more like it. What else?"

"Um, really, really hot," he said.

"Yeah, yeah, okay, what else?"

"So hot it's like Arizona."

"Okay, stop," she said, pulling her blouse back onto her shoulder. She got up off the bed and stood, buttoning her blouse. "I thought you wanted this."

"I do," he said.

"I'm gonna use the bathroom for a sec," she said, "then we can, I don't know, figure out what your deal is."

Nathaniel didn't have a deal, but he realized maybe he should come up with one.

When she returned after a couple of minutes, she sat on the bed next to him. The mattress springs squeaked. "Okay," she said. "Let's start over. Tell me what it is you like about me."

Oh, God. This is what Maggie had asked, the first time they'd almost had sex. Maggie must have been about Bridget's age. Nathaniel had stammered for an answer, blurting out the only thing he could think of—"I like you because you said yes when I asked you out"— and then pretended it was a joke, but Maggie hadn't laughed. They'd fought for days until he'd placated her with flowers and two tickets to a Gloria Estefan concert.

He'd been such a coward then. God, he'd always been a coward.

"Just now you reminded me of my wife," he said, knowing it was the wrong thing to say but saying it anyway.

Bridget frowned. "Eww."

"I don't mean you exactly. I mean your question. Look, Bridget." He stood. "I think we better call it a night."

"No kidding." She stood as well and slipped on her shoes. "I can't believe this." Her face was red with agitation. She pointed to the bed. "What just happened? Did I do something wrong?"

"No, Bridget. It's me. I'm—I'm really sorry."

"I hate it when guys say that. For what part?"

"For what part what?"

"For what part are you sorry about?"

"For all of it," he said.

"I thought you liked me."

"That's not the point."

"Are you upset I called you a bad boy? Or a nerd?"

He shook his head. "I'll pay for a room for you if you need one, if Octavio and Tammy are still, um, together."

"I don't need your money," Bridget said before she was out the door and gone.

She had made him feel like he was eighteen for one amazing moment, and then like he was thirty-eight and still the same damn person he had always been.

Nathaniel sat down on his bed and called Maggie on his cell phone.

"What, did your phone suddenly start working again?" she said.

"I've been busy here, Maggie. I'm sorry I'm not at your beck and call," he said. "I don't think you realize I'm a wanted man here. Very wanted."

"What the hell does that mean?"

"It means people are asking for me and my time. I can't just *not* show up for things. I'm a top dog now."

"Is that right?" Her rhetorical questions always made him realize how stupid he sounded.

"Look, Maggie, I said I was sorry."

"Tell that to your mother. Oh, wait, that's right, you're too 'wanted' there to have time for her."

"I called because I'm coming home." He didn't know he was until he said it out loud. "Maggie? Did you hear me?" He held the phone out to look at the screen and make sure they were still connected. When he pressed the phone again to his ear, he heard the faintest sniffles. "Maggie? You okay?" He couldn't remember the last time she had cried—ten years ago? Fifteen? Then it occurred to him that maybe she had cried, just not in front of him.

"Yeah," she said, her voice tinny and tiny.

"You sound funny. What's going on?" Nathaniel's armpits dampened.

She sniffled some more, and he could tell she was trying to cover the phone so he couldn't hear.

"Maggie?"

"Your mother's getting worse."

Nathaniel stood up. "I *am* coming home, Maggie. I promise. Now take a few deep breaths, and tell me what's happened."

She inhaled a few times. "They ran some tests and she was fine, but now she's making no sense, she's repeating herself, she's calling me Becky, she's crying for you, the kids are having meltdowns, they think Nana's dying, and I don't know, maybe she is, and I can't find a babysitter and I don't want them here but I don't want to leave your mother alone and I'm standing out here in the hallway because the nurse was kind enough to watch them for a sec but—"

"Calm down."

"You don't understand, I—"

"Stop." He waited for her to interrupt and argue back, but she didn't. "Here's what's going to happen," Nathaniel said. "You're going to go back in my mother's room and sit down and try to just breathe. Ask the nurse to get you a glass of water. As soon as we hang up, I'm calling a cab to come get you and the kids. You're not in any shape to drive. Leave your car there, get some rest. I'll bring it home in the morning after I check in on my mother. I'll catch a really early flight. Or I can just rent a car and drive. If I start before midnight, I can be there by 10 a.m." Was she breathing? "Maggie?"

"Yes." Her voice sounded as if it had been cut in half.

"Can you do what I said? Everything's gonna be okay." It's what he told his clients, and they always believed him. Sometimes he even believed it himself.

As he threw his clothes into his carry-on, he thought about calling Octavio to say goodbye, but Bridget would tell him later—if she hadn't already—what had happened. Octavio would call Nathaniel in the morning when he didn't show up for breakfast, or training, or lunch. By then Nathaniel would be home. Maybe they would both laugh it all off the next time they saw each other.

After Nathaniel called for a taxi, he waited outside the hotel. A group of three men and two women walked by him, heading inside, some joking, some chuckling. He recognized them from training, but they hadn't recognized him, or if they did, they did not bother to nod in his direction. One of the men tossed a half-eaten sandwich toward the garbage can near the entrance, but it missed and fell with a splat on the ground, bits of lettuce askew, a slice of tomato stuck to the sidewalk. The man did not return to pick it up.

Nathaniel touched his newly shaven face. He thought of Maggie's thin voice and remembered the box of condoms at the bottom of his bag. He dug out the box and tossed it into the garbage can just before the taxi pulled up. He did not miss. Nathaniel thought briefly of the things he'd learned in training, and then he thought of how awful he was, still, at calculating the value of a loss.

HAPPY

Suzette called Mig when the second plane hit the second tower. She knew he would not pick up, that later he would tell her he had been hunched in a department meeting or with one of his students or had stepped outside for a cigarette, but she punched the numbers anyway and cradled the phone against her ear until his voicemail clicked on.

"Hey, you watching the news?" she said. "It's bad, really bad."

She wondered if he would check his voicemail at all, if he was staring at a television in a colleague's office, if he wondered where she was, and whether she was safe, though it was unlike Mig to have such irrational thoughts. They were both safe in North Carolina, weren't they? Several states away from New York, but still. She wanted to hear his raspy voice, a gravel road she knew. She wanted him to say I love you. It seemed like a small thing to want on this terrible day. She wished they had purchased cell phones in August when they'd talked about it, when Mig had said he wanted one for his car.

"We just don't have the money right now," she had said, "but we will."

"We would have plenty of money if it weren't for Patricia," Mig said before picking up the remote again and tapping the volume up and up on the baseball game. There was always a baseball game.

Suzette didn't like it when Mig called Dr. Rowan "Patricia," but she didn't say a word about that. She had picked Dr. Rowan out of the list of marriage counselors based on the string of credential abbreviations trailing like children after Dr. Rowan's name, and the fact that Dr. Rowan's office sat exactly halfway between Suzette's own office and Mig's. Well, Mig liked that. He was always about halfway, taking turns cooking, splitting the check down the middle, rotating who hauled out the trash. Suzette would have made the drive all the way from Chapel Hill to his office in Raleigh had it mattered—all the way to anywhere, really. She didn't say anything about that, either.

Her office phone rang.

"Hey," Mig said when she picked up. "I can't talk now. I'm just callin' 'cause you called."

"Oh," she said, unsure what he meant, as she often was lately. One of Suzette's coworkers tapped on the door, poked her head in and whispered, "We're all downstairs if you want to join us," and left.

"It's godawful, Suze," Mig continued. "The whole humanities department is freaking out, running around the hallway."

"Has anyone heard from Lex?"

Mig's cousin had just started working in Manhattan fifteen months earlier, after graduating from college. Suzette had met Lex only once, at her and Mig's wedding three years ago. Lex had worn a suit too small for his spare body, and the sleeves, an inch short, had revealed his white cuffs and thin wrists. Not that the little suit had stopped him from getting drunk at the reception and hitting on all the single and divorced ladies, though he'd been only twenty years old.

"Mom can't get a hold of Aunt Lada," Mig said. "He's just a kid. He's gotta be okay. And anyway, Mom says Aunt Lada's always bitching at him to get the hell out of bed and get to work on time. Surely this morning was no different, right?"

"Of course. Yes. I'm sure he's fine," Suzette said, remembering how Lex had danced so furiously at their reception that he had flung his jacket off. His drenched shirt had clung to his back. "Does he even work near the Towers?"

"I don't know," Mig said. "Look, I gotta go. My class is about to start, and the students are all in a total panic. I don't know why they don't just cancel school the rest of the day. Who can focus?"

"Mig," she said. She touched one of the nicks on her wooden desk. "Mig, if they do cancel, can you come on home? I can try and get off work early. I just, I feel—"

"I don't know," he said. "We'll see."

"Okay then." She almost said I love you, but she swallowed it.

"Okay then," he said, and she wondered what he wanted to say instead.

Suzette had stopped saying I love you because in their last counseling session Mig had told Dr. Rowan, "I'm just tired of hearing it, I guess. It's like the go-to thing. It doesn't mean anything anymore."

"What do you think, Suzette?"

"I don't know," she said to Dr. Rowan, whose lips were pursed into a stitch. Her wisps of white hair reminded Suzette of a broken cobweb. "I'll have to think about that," Suzette said.

But she didn't really have to think about it. Suzette wanted Mig to say it more, but she didn't want to sound needy. She thought about the only remark her mother had ever made about Mig: "He takes up so much room." Suzette had hoped that if she herself took up less, it might finally be enough space for him.

Mig and Suzette had started seeing a marriage counselor in the middle of July, after the screen on their old 13-inch television made a fizzling sound followed by a pop. Mig had fiddled with the knobs in the back and then pumped a fist in the air. "It's dead! Finally!" He insisted that what they really needed was a larger TV anyway. "We gotta have more screen," he explained. "You can sit farther away and still catch what's going on."

At the store that night, they had stood side by side in the TV aisle, taking a few paces back to squint at the selections and tilt their heads, imagining what it would be like sitting on their futon. Was the screen wide enough? Was the picture clear? How was the color? How long would this one last?

He wanted the 32-inch, and the row of them loomed out, wide-mouthed, volume cranked. Suzette wandered one aisle over to the lone 13-inch TV, power off, humble. Mig trailed behind her. "What are you doing?"

She pointed. "I want that one."

His eyes widened. "That?"

"The 32-inch is too big." There was a whine in her voice. She stood a little straighter and said matter-of-factly, "We have a small place." She thought of the hikes they used to take, and then of Mig stretched out on the futon with the remote on sunny afternoons.

"You can't be serious. This is what we've had," he said, wagging a finger at the TV, scolding the innocent appliance, "for three whole years."

"It works. It's all we need."

He shook his head but squatted down and grabbed the box from the bottom shelf. He didn't look up at her when he said, "Happy?"

In the evening on September 11, Mig didn't come home early or on time. At 6 p.m., Suzette flipped on the TV and slipped off her black flats and took a few steps toward the galley kitchen, right off the living room, to listen to the news from there, but then she turned around and moved no further. The pair of shoes dangled from her hand. After a minute, she sat on the edge of the futon and stared at their little TV's face. She slid down to the floor in front of the 13-inch, turned off the volume, and stared at the black smoke frothing from the first tower, and the second plane slicing through the second tower and blowing out the other side, the same images over and over. Powdered people, screaming people. The world felt, for the second time in her life, as if it were swirling down a small but inevitable silver drain.

Suzette forgot she was hungry, as she often did. It was easier to remember other people's hunger than her own.

The first tragedy Suzette endured had happened four and half years ago, in winter, when she still lived in Boston. Of course it had been a small, personal tragedy, not set on a worldwide stage, yet even small tragedies can leave rubble in a heart.

She and Mig had been dating only two months when Suzette's mother called from Buffalo and said, "You need to come home. Now." Suzette's father, who had been ill for years, had taken a turn for the worse. Suzette, who owned no car and could find no flight, was frantically checking train schedules when Mig showed up at her apartment, for once without his car keys jangling around in his pockets. He gestured with his thumb toward the street. "Car's running," he said. "Let's go."

He drove the whole seven hours, stopping only once to dash into the restroom and then bust back out while zipping up his jeans. He gunned the car ten, fifteen, and every once in a while twenty miles over the limit, and though any other day Suzette would have protested, on that particular day, with its chunks of dirty ice and grimacing sky, she felt only immense gratitude for his boldness.

When they pulled up to her parents' blue Victorian, Mig said, "It's okay. You go. I'll wait right here," and let her rush alone into the house. He sat in the car for an hour until she emerged again and tapped on the frosted window, her face glistening with sadness.

"Come inside," she said. "At least you can meet my mother."

Mig had remained with them those five days—for the wake, the funeral, the casseroles, the bleating phone, the shaking of friends' and strangers' hands—days Suzette remembered as fragile and uncertain, her mother's face a pale gray. Suzette told Mig he didn't have to stay, but she was relieved when he did.

On all of her childhood nights, her father had been the parent who tucked her into bed and kissed her forehead. He'd been the one to clap his hands at her victories, shake his head at her losses, the one who told her, "You are the brightest star in my every sky." Without her father, who had made the world tolerable, everything felt hollow, even the house, and the words she and her mother spoke to each other cast long shadows of what they would never dare say out loud: *Why are you the one still here?*

Mig's presence, bulky and honest, had made it bearable. Wearing a wool hat, he slept on the rickety daybed on her parents' three-season porch. His feet hung off the edge. He did not complain, not about the bed, the chilly porch, nor the fact that Suzette's mother barely spoke to him, only nodded toward him when he addressed her.

During those five days, Suzette did not sleep. On the night that they returned to the city, long after midnight, Mig trudged behind her up the stairs to her apartment, and at the doorway said, "Want me to stay?"

She had not dared to ask, after all he'd done, and—in the way that she did when trying not to impose—she did not say all of what she wanted, only half. "For a little while."

Mig did not take off his clothes or even his coat; he lay on top of her comforter, one arm flung around her. Before he dozed off, he looked at her and said, "I'm so sorry, Suze. Death's a bitch." And this had made her laugh.

Although as he breathed deeply into the night, Mig stretched, widening the space he inhabited and taking over the bed, Suzette, now only in a corner, pulled her legs to her chest, shifted up against him, and for the first time since her mother had called, slept until morning.

◆◆◆

On September 11, Mig bungled through the door at 8 p.m. with his messenger bag hanging halfway down his arm.

"Hey," Suzette said, getting up off the floor. "You okay?"

"No word about Lex."

"Really?" She walked over to him and lifted the weighted bag off his arm.

"Don't do that." He took the big canvas bag from her hands. "I got it." He plunked it on the floor and rifled through the bag she had bought him two years ago when he had started teaching at the community college. He was searching for something in the bag, but then he stopped, nothing in his hands. "Did you check the machine? Did Lex call?"

"Lex doesn't have our number, does he?" Suzette said. "But I can check—"

"Damn it." He stomped up their carpeted stairs toward the machine. Suzette felt each thump, each muffled step away.

The couch in Dr. Rowan's office was hard, like a plank, and covered in a mottled fabric that scratched Suzette's legs. She and Mig called the couch "the itchy omen." They had other words for these sessions— Mig referred to them as "the hours of reckoning"—a shared vocabulary based on fright and nervousness. They named Dr. Rowan's pen, which she sometimes tapped after writing down a note, "the metronome of doom." They called her notebook "the little hate book," and the sound spa she set outside her door "the whirl of worries." Suzette liked it when they joked about it together, but sometimes Mig didn't find any of it funny.

"Why the hell do we need therapy?" he had asked Suzette more than once. "I feel like a fucking sideshow."

She wanted to say, "I don't know if you love me anymore," but instead she said, "I think we just need help sorting some things out."

A mirror hung on one side of Dr. Rowan's office so that when you entered or left, you caught your reflection in what Suzette thought of as "the truth teller." She didn't ever call it that to Mig.

In the mirror's reflection, she could see him looking down at the carpet, his brown shaggy hair hanging over his face as he slumped in and out of their hours of reckoning. His bag dragged down, huge and heavy, on his slack shoulders. In her own reflection, which she caught in glances, she saw her eyes rounded in shock, and her hair (pulled too tightly into her slight and nameless-brown ponytail) appeared plastered to her head.

During the sessions, Suzette sometimes sweated behind her knees and under her arms, even though Dr. Rowan's office exuded a steady, airy coolness. On those days, Suzette kept her elbows glued to her sides in case her armpits smelled bad, and she used only her forearms and hands to gesture, which meant she mostly did not move at all. Afterward, she thought about all the awful things Mig said: "I hate my job," "I'm dying to get to a bigger city," and worst of all, "I'm suffocating."

At the end of their counseling session the week before September 11, Dr. Rowan had suggested they try a homework assignment. Mig had glared at Suzette, and she pretended not to notice, reaching down to scratch her leg.

"I want you each to write out a list of the things you love about the other person."

"How many things?" Mig asked. "Top three? Top five?"

"As many as you want," Dr. Rowan said. "I want you to really spend some time thinking about the qualities that make Suzette special to you."

"Fuck," he said under his breath.

Dr. Rowan leaned forward. "What's that?"

"Fine," Mig said.

"Good. And Suzette, are you clear about the assignment?"

"Yes, Dr. Rowan."

Afterward, on the way to their separate cars, Mig snickered, "*Yes, Dr. Rowan. We do anything you say, Dr. Rowan.*"

"Stop it, Mig."

"I'm just joking."

"It's not funny."

"C'mon, Suze."

"That's our marriage in there."

"No." Mig grabbed Suzette's arm to make her stop walking. "*Patricia's* not our marriage." He pointed back and forth to Suzette and to himself. "*This* is our marriage."

Exactly, Suzette thought. *That's the problem.*

The evening following their counseling session, Mig had started a list in his head right away, but not the one Patricia had asked for. This list was of all the things that annoyed him about Suzette. He wasn't an idiot. He had known from the start the point of the exercise was for Suzette to hear how much he loved her, but he more easily thought of the things that irked him:

—*Talks too softly.* He had to strain to listen to her sometimes. He hated straining. It reminded him of toilets.

—*Has too many teeth.* Well, it wasn't that she had too many, it was that they were too big. Her mouth seemed crowded.

—*Has flat hair.* He would admit this to no one, but he loved perms from the '80s that by now had long gone out of style. He liked fluffy bigness, which went against his whole value system of minimal and earthy. He wanted to like the looks of the women who picketed and attended rallies beside him—women with cropped cuts or spiky ends, or with their hair just plain pulled back—but he didn't. He liked big and bad and curly.

—*Picks at her food.* Really, the picking only bothered him now that she was too scrawny. *Too scrawny* would be next on his list, if he were writing it down, which he wasn't dumb enough to do. She had been meatier when he'd met her and in their first two years of marriage, but over the last year she had lost weight, begun stabbing at her food like she was attacking it. "For crying out loud, just eat it," he told her, but she never listened to his advice anymore.

—*The way she stays up half the night making job search plans for her clients and then complains in the morning how tired she is.* Well, okay, she didn't exactly complain. She took sips from his mug of coffee, so he'd offer to make Suzette her own coffee in her own mug, and she'd say, "No, no, I don't need any," but it seemed like she'd sip at least half of his. Or maybe it was only a little, but why couldn't she drink her own goddamned coffee from her own mug?

—*Refuses to move.* This was the most egregious on his list. He could live with all the other things—in fact, he was sure they would annoy him a lot less—if they just lived somewhere else, a bigger city in a more urban setting in the North, where they belonged. The South sucked. And yeah, she had moved here for his job, a great teaching job in the philosophy department at a high-ranking university, and though it hadn't been tenure-track it might have turned into that, but he'd lost it after two semesters—*two semesters*—and he wanted to believe it was really because of the funding cuts like they'd said, but he'd seen the comments on his student evaluations: "arrogant asshole,"

"I would have been better off just reading the book," "yawn." And now that Suzette loved her work at The Women's Center, he was stuck at the low-level, low-wage, mind-numbing community college. He was meant for better things.

On September 11, Mig had known long before he drove home that Suzette wouldn't touch food—she freaked out and her stomach closed in a crisis—so he had stopped off I-40 at McDonald's and sat alone, swiveling from left to right in one of its yellow chairs while chomping on a Big Mac. Suzette never ate fast food, and that evening, as the world swelled and darkened, spiraling out of control, all he craved was a greasy burger. Better yet, two. One for him, one for Lex.

When Mig got home, he wasn't just full: he felt sick.

"Did you eat already?" Suzette asked after he checked the empty answering machine. She was sitting cross-legged with her back against the futon. The TV was silent, and the images burned across the screen.

"We should have gotten those damn cell phones," he said.

"Want the volume on?"

"I can hear it," he said, and he knew she understood what he meant.

At 9 p.m. on September 11, Mig got the call from his mother.

"He's fine." She was crying and laughing. "Your idiot of a cousin overslept so badly, Lada had to wake him up to give him the news. Thank God," she said and wept. "Thank God."

Mig held the phone tighter and put his head in his hands. He wasn't close to his young cousin, but Lex's little rebellions—letting an errant cuss word fly in front of their grandmother, or slinking in, long after prayer, for a holiday meal—had always reminded Mig of himself. But only in some ways. Later, after he'd hung up with his mother, Mig remembered how hugely relieved Lada had been when Lex graduated college, especially after he almost got suspended for smoking marijuana. Or rather, for getting caught. What kind of idiot gets caught smoking dope when all you have to do is keep your door shut and your window open? In the end, Lex always seemed to escape. Today, his carelessness had basically engineered a sort of miracle.

Lucky son of a bitch, Mig thought while he smoked a cigarette out on their creaky deck. Did he even know how lucky he was?

◆◆◆

Suzette fell asleep on the futon just before midnight, her back to Mig. He had pulled out the old futon to lay it flat and turned off all the lights so only the television's glow flashed onto their faces. Now the images told the story only to him. Suzette had broken free from the beast of a day, and he felt glad of it. Her palms were pressed together, as if she were praying, and her mouth was slightly ajar.

He closed his eyes and began the list:

—*Laughs at my jokes.* Sometimes he could make her double over with laughter. She would say, "Stop, Mig. My face hurts too much." That hadn't happened in a long time.

—*Has great skin.* She was pale, sure, but he liked that, and she never got all dry and cracked the way he did. And she had that scattering of freckles across her face that appeared only in summer. It would be disappearing soon.

—*Smells like books.* She didn't smell like a musty old book, but like a new one that only faintly smelled of ink. He trusted books more than he trusted people.

—*Makes the best sourdough bread.* It tasted nearly sweet. She was a better baker than he was. She made braided challah bread, soft pretzels sprinkled with kosher salt, and the best lemon bars with a thin film of confectioners sugar. She was also a master of what he thought of as reincarnating foods, making one thing turn into something else: milk into yogurt and cheese, cucumbers into pickles, cabbage into sauerkraut. She had the patience to wait for things to turn, a patience he'd never had.

Shit. Now he was thinking of the other things, the things he didn't want to talk about to Patricia. He shut his eyes.

—*Doesn't nag me about my smoking, though she hates it.* He'd quit when they decided to get married, but after losing the job, he went directly to a 7-Eleven. "You smell like smoke," she'd said once, just after he started up again. But that was it, as if she'd decided to step over a pile of crap and pretend it wasn't there.

—*Never once made me feel like an idiot for losing that university job, even though she had every right to.* He had dreaded telling her when he got canned, had kept it to himself for days until finally he couldn't take the loneliness of it, even at the cost of the embarrassment of this failure. "So what?" she had said with a shrug, to his utter relief. "There'll be others."

—*Can see me.* This could have gone on his Things-that-Annoy-Me-about-Suzette list. He could be a real asshole sometimes, and he knew she was paying attention. She saw every eye roll, heard every exasperated sigh, and she probably sensed things she couldn't actually know, like how he made a point to step out of his office building and smoke when his colleague—beautiful (big hair, wide hips), sassy, sarcastic as hell—was already leaning back against the brick wall, taking a drag on her cancer stick. God he loved to watch that woman lift her head and exhale, but after a while, his skin would get all creepy-crawly and he'd head back inside because he would think of Suzette and how she would probably ask later how his day was, and it would feel like no matter what he answered, she could see all *this* in his expression. Sometimes he just wanted space. Sometimes he wished Suzette were not so savvy, not so alert, not noticing him all the goddamn time. But she'd always seen him, even back at the beginning, and still wanted him. It was why he'd trusted her love in the first place.

Mig glanced over at Suzette beside him and wondered what her her list would look like—not the one for Patricia but Suzette's Things-I-Hate-about-My-Douchebag-Husband list.

He closed his eyes and thought of moths, swarms of them fluttering in a gray cloud, out of windows, out of hallways, out of her open mouth.

Mig did not rise from the futon until the sun gashed through the windows. He had not changed out of his clothes from yesterday, so now he was more crumpled and disheveled than usual as he made coffee. Not that he cared, but he thought about what Suzette would see as she sat up, which she was doing now, yawning and rubbing her eyes.

"Hey," he said, lifting up his white mug. "Want some?"

She shook her head and turned to the TV, which Mig had clicked off hours ago. "Is it still true?" she asked, her voice a whisper. "Tell me it was all a bad dream."

"I'm calling in sick today or canceling my classes or something," he said and started up the coffee bean grinder. It roared and spewed inside the clear plastic lid. He dropped the ground coffee into the filter lining the pour-over brewer.

"I'm going to work," she said. She was still staring at the blank TV.

"We have that appointment with Patricia." He lifted the kettle and tilted it. Hot water plunged into the brewer. "You know, the whole luuuuuv list thing. Is that at ten?"

"I'm canceling," she said.

"Seriously, Suze. Is it at ten?"

"I'm not going."

"Too many things you love about me?" He kept his voice steady, but his mouth and throat felt dry, as if he had swallowed chalk and dust. He coughed and reached for the sugar. "Need more time for my list?"

She reached for her shoes.

"Suze, what is it?"

She slid her feet into them.

"The world just blew up," he said. "People are dying. What is it?"

Her gaze did not stray from the empty face of the TV when she said, "You don't make me happy anymore."

"Happy?" Mig swallowed and turned again to his mug still on the counter. He stirred the crystals into the mug's open mouth. He did not lift his eyes from the swirling coffee. The spoon clanged against the ceramic, the sound a final bell. "Love isn't about happiness, Suzette," he said. "It's about survival." He walked over to his wife, who was still sitting on the futon, and handed her his white mug. "Here, have some, or have all of it—if for no one else, then for Dr. Rowan," he said. "It's gonna be a long morning."

THE COUNTRY OF MARRIAGE

The first time Suzette saw Lonnie Newman, it was early March at a PTA meeting. He sat, legs crossed, five chairs down from her in the circle. His pocket watch dangled from his belt loop, swinging back and forth. The chain glinted under the classroom's fluorescent lights.

"Welcome, welcome, Lonnie Newman!" said Miss DeWitt, the third-grade teacher who ran the meetings. "Let's everyone give a round of applause to our newest member." Lonnie gave a little wave and then uncrossed his legs and turned red as the PTA clapped.

Lonnie wore an oxford shirt, along with jeans and Birkenstocks with brown socks. He had a full beard and his hair was pulled back into a long, thin ponytail, and in his right hand he held a handkerchief, which he used to swipe at his nose now and again. Lonnie sneezed throughout that meeting, just as he would later in every meeting until late May, always making Suzette wish to offer him a tissue and to rub his back, the way she did for her five-year-old daughter, Lena, the way Suzette had once tried to do with Mig when they were first married, until Mig had jerked away and said, "Stop it. You're making me itch."

On the day Lonnie first showed up at PTA, Suzette and Mig were newly separated, not that anyone knew but her best friend and coworker, Flavia. Suzette had not even told her mother. She dreaded the call, not because her mother liked Mig but because Suzette didn't want to give her mother the satisfaction. Suzette still wore her wedding ring, a narrow gold band with barely enough room for the inside inscription that bore the date of their marriage and the word "Always." Separation did not mean divorce, after all. Suzette was just as her father had been about anything gone wrong—ever the optimist that things might take a turn for the better.

Lonnie was the only single dad in the PTA (there were at least eleven unmarried moms, most of them divorced). Suzette knew this because on the day any new member joined, Miss DeWitt passed out a new parent roster on pale pink paper with a list of all their names and contact information. Miss DeWitt used a code in parentheses by everyone's name: D for divorced, S for single, M for married. Suzette didn't know why they needed to have their marital status screaming from the page. Suzette had an M in the parentheses by her name, as did Mig, who was on the roster even though he had not shown up in over six months.

When Suzette got home to the condominium, Mig's car was parked in one of the two spots marked 106C, their number, or what had been their number until Mig moved out nineteen days ago. The condo windows were brightly lit—upstairs, downstairs, all over the place— a thing that used to bother Suzette, who snapped off lamps and switches behind everyone. Now she found that, when alone with Lena, she kept everything on. As she opened the front door, Lena squealed and ran right past her—"Hi, Mommy!"—and up the stairs, Mig a few feet behind, chasing her but clearly not in any hurry.

"Hey," he said to Suzette before ascending the stairs, calling out to Lena, "I'm gonna find you and tickle you!" He trudged one step at a time. Mig always trudged.

"Did you all eat dinner already?" Suzette asked.

Mig's footsteps thudded above as he pretended to search for Lena, who always hid beneath their bed—or what had been their bed. Suzette set her bag down on the kitchen counter. There in the sink, two big bowls, a spoon and a splash of milk in each. So they'd had cereal for dinner. Again. "I left a casserole in the fridge!" she called up the stairs, but just then Mig shouted, "Gotcha!" and Lena began another torrent of squeals.

This place was too small for the three of them anyway. Suzette had been trying for years to convince Mig it was perfectly fine, but now she felt as if every room could barely accommodate them. In reality, their Chapel Hill condo had been just big enough for Suzette and Mig—and at the top end of their budget—and they had planned on getting a bigger place, a bigger townhome or maybe a two-bedroom house in Durham or Hillsborough since Chapel Hill prices were outrageous, but with her nonprofit salary and his teaching job, they just couldn't swing it. And anyway, Suzette loved the kitchen with its yellow walls and white appliances, everything sunny-side up. Suzette was grateful they hadn't purchased anything bigger, even though Mig called the place "the fat man's squeeze." At least she and Lena could stay here if things didn't get better.

Lena pattered down the stairs and threw her arms around Suzette. "Mommy! He found me!"

"He did," Suzette said.

Mig lumbered down the stairs but did not come into the kitchen. He stood by the front door, lifting his coat off the doorknob of the hall closet and slipping his arms into the sleeves.

"Thanks for picking her up and staying with her," Suzette said. She didn't know exactly why she was thanking him. Flavia always told her, "He's her parent, too. You don't have to be so grateful." But Suzette wanted him to know she appreciated it all, especially now that he had to make the extra trip to and from his apartment in Durham.

"Where are you going?" Lena asked Mig. She went to him and held his hand. "Why are you leaving?"

Mig and Suzette looked at each other. Were they doing this all wrong?

"Do you want to stay?" Suzette asked him.

Mig crouched down to Lena. "I'll pick you up tomorrow from school, like always. I promise."

Suzette turned away as Lena hugged Mig. She opened the fridge and withdrew the casserole dish, white ceramic with glass lid, a note taped on top of it that read, "Heat for 20 minutes at 350. Add grated cheese if you want." She ripped off the note and dished out a heap of cold casserole for herself.

The second time Suzette saw Lonnie Newman was at another PTA meeting. He sat by himself, an empty chair on either side of him, and he didn't say much of anything; neither did Suzette. He didn't contribute new ideas or argue for or against the proposed craft fair fundraiser, but as other meetings passed, Suzette kept noticing him. He was nothing like Mig, was more like Suzette, so quiet he receded. Suzette was used to paying attention to the softer, subtler, even unspoken things in people:

the way someone might cast a look off to the right before answering a question perceived to be tough, the way a person might stand up straighter when searching for courage. Suzette preferred watching people over arguing or making waves. When Mig had attended PTA (which he had done only three times), he interrupted other parents and sighed and folded his arms across his chest when he disagreed with something. He stopped going because, he said, no one was capable of making a single decision unless everyone was happy. "Which means nothing ever happens because when is everyone happy?" he said.

Suzette was one of the ones who wanted everyone happy, and who, when making a suggestion—a motion to stock the vending machines with only healthful snacks or a move to incorporate composting into the cafeteria kitchen—would follow the suggestion with a glance around the room to see if other parents were nodding.

"I filed the paperwork," Mig said when Suzette answered her phone at work. Mig was in New Jersey with Lena for a few days over Lena's spring break.

"So they said it was okay?" Suzette asked, picking lint off her slacks. "They" was New Jersey.

"I didn't tell them I don't live here," he said. "I gave them Uncle Mel's address."

Suzette rubbed her shoes against the carpet, shuffling them as if she were gliding forward, except she was seated and going nowhere. Outside her second-floor office window, the bare tree was beginning to green.

"When will it be done?" Suzette asked.

"You should get a copy of the complaint," Mig said. "You'll have to sign it and fill out some paperwork and send it back. After that, six to eight weeks, so they say."

"We could just do this in North Carolina," she offered. North Carolina law said you had to be separated for a year before you could file. Mig said that was too long. It wasn't the first time she had made the suggestion that they stick with North Carolina law without actually asking him why he was in such a hurry. Today he didn't say his usual, "I heard you the first time."

"Some of the paperwork can be confusing," he said instead. "Uncle Mel helped me. If you need help—"

"I won't need help." Clouds blew across the sun, making the day seem rainy when it wasn't.

"Is Flavia at the office today?" he asked.

Well, there was that. Suzette knew that Mig knew that Flavia would hold Suzette's hand if she needed it.

"Maybe," Suzette said. Flavia was definitely there.

"Okay," he said. "I better get back to Lena. Uncle Mel is trying to teach her how to play poker, but he's using M&M'S for chips. She's basically eating them as they go."

"When are you coming home again?" Suzette asked, though she knew exactly when. "I miss her so much."

"Yeah. I know," Mig said. "I'm really sorry, Suzette." But for what all he was apologizing, she couldn't really tell.

The fifth time Suzette saw Lonnie Newman was at the craft fair in the school gym at the end of May. Lena was threading macaroni onto a long red piece of yarn to make a necklace, and Suzette was standing on tiptoe, trying to peer over the crowd to see if there was a line at the face-painting table—her idea—in hopes it would be a good moneymaker.

A soft male voice beside her said, "Did you lose someone?" There stood Lonnie, holding the hand of a lanky little girl with straight blonde hair held on one side in a purple barrette.

"Hi," Suzette said.

"Do you need help?" he asked Suzette. He said to the little girl, "Naomi, this is Suzette." So he knew Suzette's name. "We're in PTA together. And Suzette, this is my angel, Naomi."

"I'm not an angel," Naomi said. "I'm a girl." She pointed to the table where Lena was working, engrossed in her necklace. "Can I make something, too?" she asked.

"Of course." He dug some money from his jeans pocket. "How much is it?"

Naomi turned to the poster set on an easel that listed the prices. It was sprinkled with glitter. "A bracelet is just $1.50," she said, "but I want to make a necklace. That's $3.00."

Lonnie handed her a five.

"Don't worry. I'll keep the change," she said. She walked to the far end of the table and began instructing the woman taking the money on what color yarn she wanted and how thick.

Lonnie smiled at Suzette. "Sometimes I wonder if she's actually my seven-year-old kid or my seventeen-year-old boss."

"I know that feeling. Lena just turned six, and I swear she thinks she's a teenager."

Lonnie smiled again. So much of his face was sheltered by his bushy beard. It looked bristly, but perhaps it was really soft and smooth. "Hey, I'm sorry," he said, "earlier you were looking for someone. Did you need help? Did I interrupt?"

"I was checking out the face painting. I'd feel terrible if it were a flop. I'm the one who came up with the idea."

"It's gonna be great," Lonnie said. "I saw a long line when we went by a few minutes ago."

"Oh good." The gymnasium was loud and starting to get muggy. Two boys sprinted by, one of them holding a rainbow kite, which thwapped Suzette in the forehead as they passed.

"Slow down," Lonnie said, but the boys were long gone, and Lonnie's voice was too soft to reach them. "You okay?"

"I'm fine," she said.

"Good." He stood there smiling at her.

She put a hand to her forehead, which was throbbing a little. "Mig always says . . ."

"Who's Mig?"

Mig was technically her husband, but the word felt jagged now in her mouth. Flavia had been telling her she needed to start practicing: "Add the 'ex.' *Ex*-husband. *Ex*-husband." But what did Flavia know about ex-husbands? She was married with twin toddlers. Her family was intact.

Miss DeWitt appeared as if out of nowhere wearing a stoplight-red dress with black polka dots. She was holding a printed floor plan of the gym. "Hey, you two! Good to see you here. Where's your husband?" she asked Suzette. Lonnie raised his eyebrows. "Or is he going to miss this, too?"

"He's not my . . ." Suzette cleared her throat.

"I know, I know," said Miss DeWitt with a wave of her hand. "I didn't think he was yours to watch over or mind. I was joking. Mostly. But it would be nice if he showed up every once in a while to something. Or if he returned my calls."

"You called him?" Suzette's skin felt warm and prickly.

"He didn't tell you? Oh my. You two need to communicate more. I call all delinquent parents," Miss DeWitt said. "The dads especially sometimes need a little extra push. Not you, Lonnie, of course." She fanned herself with the floor plan. "You've been great, especially doing all this setup with me last night. I needed your muscles and can't thank you enough."

"No worries." Lonnie took a couple of steps toward his daughter.

"If you don't mind," Miss DeWitt said to Suzette, "I'd really love your help getting Mig more involved. We need more from him."

"I'm gonna go," Lonnie said. "Nice to see you both." He wandered off.

Miss DeWitt watched him go, still fanning herself. "I wish all of them were like Lonnie Newman. Don't you?"

The seventh time Suzette saw Lonnie Newman was in late June, on a Friday night when Mig had taken Lena to a Durham Bulls baseball game. Suzette and Flavia had decided to get a drink after work at the West End Wine Bar as soon as they learned that a large grant had fallen through for their nonprofit employer. They were sitting on couches by the front windows when Lonnie walked by holding hands with Naomi. Holding Naomi's other hand was a woman with a halo of frizzy blonde hair and a nose ring, one of those little hoops that reminded Suzette of something you wanted to tug on.

"What is it?" Flavia asked. She set her wine glass on the low table in front of them and leaned toward the window to see what Suzette saw. "You know them?"

"Sort of. He's in PTA." Lonnie and the woman were not talking, but Naomi was. Suzette asked, "Do you think they look happy?"

"I don't know." Flavia said. "Maybe. Why?"

"Just curious."

"Hm." That's what Flavia said when she wanted to say more but was holding back.

"What? Just say it."

"Nothing. Really." Flavia picked up her wine once more. "It's just that in all the years I've known you, I've never really seen you check out a guy."

"I wasn't checking him out."

"Of course you weren't," Flavia said with a smile. "What? I didn't say anything."

In early August, Mig and Suzette were standing side by side, watching Lena swim in a meet. She wriggled down the lane in her yellow swimsuit and wore a swim cap that was robin-egg blue, the color of the beginnings of things but also the shade of an ocean at the end of a day. Suzette and Mig had arrived at the same time in the parking lot to show Lena she could count on both of them, and they had settled next to each other on the bleachers. Every time Lena swam, they both stood, not caring whom they blocked.

After Lena finished her third event—she came in second to last in her one-length heat—Mig said in a low voice, "Thanks for making this easy."

"What are you talking about?"

"You know, the divorce thing."

It wasn't just a thing. Suzette pushed up on her sunglasses, which kept slipping down. "It isn't easy."

"That's what I mean. You're holding it together."

Suzette didn't know whether to feel complimented or insulted, but it was not the first time she didn't know how to feel, or she felt too many things at once, and she was never any good at articulating emotions on the spot. "We have Lena," she said.

The smell of chlorine invaded everything even though they were outside, even though the air had total freedom.

"I know," Mig said. "I don't want this to be hard for her."

"But it is."

"I'm sorry. I really am. This isn't what I wanted for her."

The metal bleachers felt hard and sticky, and Suzette shifted.

"Sometimes I don't know what I'm doing," Mig said.

Suzette didn't want to talk about this here, at Lena's meet. She just wanted to clap and focus on who made it first or last to the end of the lane. She picked up her purse and rummaged through it for some ChapStick or a tissue or her wallet.

"You know what I mean?" he said. "I think I've finally figured things out, and then . . ." He made a hand gesture like something was exploding, but he had been the one to bomb it all.

Suzette got up, purse in her grasp. Mig looked up at her with those big, copper-brown eyes. They were like coins worth something in the country of marriage but now valueless in her own. "Where are you going?" he asked, the same question she had been wanting to ask him for six months.

"To get a bottle of water." She almost asked if he wanted anything, but she pushed past him and walked away.

In September, Suzette saw Lonnie Newman for the eighth time, at the first PTA meeting of the year. His beard was shorn, his ponytail cut off. He was wearing a plaid, short-sleeved collared shirt and cargo shorts. He stopped in front of Suzette's chair. "How was your summer?" he asked.

"Well," she said, trying to figure out how honest to be, "it was a bit of a rollercoaster."

"Really? Mine, too. And I get sick on rollercoasters."

She laughed.

"Hope things slowed down for you," he said.

She nodded, and he took his place across the circle but did not look her way again for the rest of the meeting.

The envelope was so thick the papers seemed to want to bust out of their enclosure. Suzette knew what it was, posted from New Jersey four days prior. She stuffed it into her bag and opened the front door of the condo. The television, a wee 13-inch, was on, the evening news playing. Mig and Lena were eating peanut butter and crackers on the couch.

"Mommy!" Lena ran to her and threw her little arms around Suzette.

"Hey, baby." Suzette inhaled the strawberry scent of Lena's hair. "How was school?"

"I learned more Spanish."

"Is that right?"

"*Me llamo* Lena."

"What does that mean?"

Lena scrunched up her nose, considering. Then she smiled. "I am Lena, and I am strong."

"Wow," Suzette said, "that's a lot of English words. You sure that's what it means?"

"Yep."

"It doesn't mean 'I am strong,' Lena," Mig said from the couch.

"Yes it does."

"We went over this just five minutes ago."

"You don't know what it means," Lena said. "You weren't there." Tears appeared.

"It's okay, sweetie," Suzette said. "How about you run upstairs and get me the Berenstain Bears book, and I'll read it to you before dinner."

"I don't like that book anymore."

"You don't?"

"I'm too old for it."

"Then get whatever book you want, okay?"

Lena nodded and ran upstairs.

"That isn't what it means," Mig said. "She's just mad at me."

"For what?"

"Who knows? She's six."

"Well, I have it under control here if you want to take off," Suzette said.

"Didn't you say you needed to go to the store before coming home?"

"I already did."

"Want me to help bring in the bags?"

"No," she said. "I've got it."

Mig stood, brushing the crumbs off his pants and onto the carpet. "Oh, sorry."

"I'll get it later."

"Right. Well, then." Mig grabbed his keys off the counter. "See you tomorrow."

Lena rushed down the stairs, waving a book at Suzette. "This one, this one."

"I'm heading out, honey," he said to Lena. "You wanna say goodbye?"

"Bye," she said, already sitting at the kitchen table, already peeling open her book.

Lonnie Newman rarely said a word in meetings, but when he did, he raised his hand. Suzette liked how polite he was, that he waited for his turn. She could tell he was a rule follower, as was she, and so it wasn't until seven and a half months after Lonnie had first shown up, and ten days after a New Jersey judge declared Suzette and Mig divorced, that she worked up the nerve to finally say to Lonnie, "Do you happen to know of a place around here to get a good cup of coffee?" She had practiced this for an entire three days—Flavia had given her the line and made Suzette promise to use it.

"I don't drink coffee," Lonnie said before some sort of realization passed across his face, igniting it along the way. "I'm sorry. I don't know why I just said that. I thought you were married."

Suzette's neck and face grew hot and nettled. "I was."

"What I mean to say is I drink tea. I can order tea," Lonnie said. "Do you know of a place that has tea and coffee? Wait, you just asked me." He was starting to sweat. "I can find a place. Do you want me to find a place?"

"Yes," she said. "I do."

◆◆◆

Suzette and Mig decided they would hold on to the condo—that is, Suzette would live in it with Lena. This way, her young life would be disrupted as little as possible. Under the circumstances. Suzette and Mig would sell it in a year or two or three, split the profits then. Mig said he hoped it would be sooner rather than later. Until that time, they would split the payments for the mortgage and the rent for his studio apartment in downtown Durham. This was fair, wasn't it? Suzette didn't want to pay for his drab, unkempt, window-less cell of an apartment (okay, it wasn't really that awful—it had white walls and several windows, just never enough), but she was raised to be polite and sensible and reasonable. She was raised to keep her cool.

On a Saturday morning, three hours before Suzette was going to pick up Lena from Mig's, she arrived at Foster's Market, a place Suzette had been to a dozen times before, mostly when her mother came to visit so that together they could pick up exactly what she wanted to eat. This was easier than trying to guess her mother's ever-changing taste and getting it wrong. Suzette and Mig had come here once for coffee when they had first moved to Chapel Hill, in the years before Lena, but Mig had preferred Cafe Driadde with its more austere inside. "More authentic," Mig said. He thought Foster's Market was too uppity, and Suzette had not thought much of it until now that she was seated waiting for Lonnie Newman to show. She disagreed with Mig and set her purse to the side and leaned back into one of the couches, exhaling and relaxing for the first time in months. She closed her eyes. The chatter from other customers rose and bounced off the ceiling and walls, and she inhaled the smell of baked goods—her own specialty when it came to the kitchen.

"Been waiting long?"

Suzette opened her eyes, and there was Lonnie, standing over her.

"You look beautiful," he said.

"I didn't know you were here," she said. "I'm sorry."

"I just got here, and this is perfect."

Suzette grabbed her purse and put her hand on the couch to push herself up, but Lonnie said, "Stay here. I'll get you what you want."

"Really?"

"Is that okay? I'd love to treat you, but if you're not comfortable with that, we can—"

"Yes. That's great."

"Good." he said. "Super. Now, what would you like?"

"A small coffee and a croissant, please."

"Coming right up."

Lonnie would later confess he was eager to pay because he had wanted to show her how glad he was that they were finally doing this but he didn't want her to think that he in any way thought she wasn't capable of paying her own way. She liked that his earnestness came with a compliment. (Mig would have rolled his eyes at all of it—he was a slap-cash-down sort of guy, no questions asked).

Over one coffee and one black tea, one croissant, one order of sourdough toast with lots of butter, and one peanut butter cookie, which they split, Lonnie asked Suzette about where she was from originally, about her family, about her work at The Women's Center where she counseled women on finding careers and job searching, and about what she liked to do in her free time. *What free time?* she thought, but she answered that she loved walking in the woods, which she used to do and maybe still loved, and reading, which she sometimes indulged in after Lena went to bed and before Suzette nodded off.

"What about you?" she asked. She wanted to know everything, a feeling she hadn't had in so long that finding it again—feeling it again—seemed like dusting off a chest shoved in the back of a closet, but a chest you hadn't given away because you knew one day you might need to unlock it again.

Lonnie talked about his garden: he had built a raised bed he used all year round, growing spinach throughout winter under plastic hoops he had fashioned himself. He collected vintage games—Battleship, Connect Four, Sorry—sometimes bribing Naomi to play them with him, but he was having to pony up better bribes. ("Offering to let her make a call on my flip phone isn't working anymore.") And he played the violin, although he admitted he was rusty.

"I used to play gigs with Naomi's mom, back when we were together. She plays guitar. Beautifully," Lonnie added. "We called ourselves the Sweet Tones."

"Nice name," Suzette said, taking the last sip of her coffee.

"It was good while it lasted."

"When did you divorce?"

"We never got married," he said. "Lindy didn't believe in marriage. She believed in open relationships."

"You mean, open open?"

Lonnie smiled. "Yes, that kind," he said. "I know it's a little weird."

"No, I mean, I've heard of it, but I've just never met anyone who's tried it."

"Now you have," he said. "If you want to ask me something about it, you can."

Suzette shifted on the couch. She had a million questions. "Were you happy?"

"You mean, being in an open relationship? When it was theoretical, sure, but not in reality."

"What did reality look like?"

"A guy named Bart who drove a black Ford F-350 and smoked cigars."

"Oh," Suzette said. "So you didn't have a ... ?"

"Nope," he said. "I was never interested in anyone but Lindy. I'm a one-woman type of man. At least one at a time."

"You don't believe in a single soul mate for every person?"

"No way," he said. "Do you?"

"Not anymore. I'm sure I once did, until the person I thought was my one soul mate stopped wanting to be my soul mate. What else is there to do but hope there is another?"

On their second date, the following Saturday, Lonnie took Suzette's hand as they walked in Duke Gardens, but as he did, he lifted it and asked, "This okay?" Permission. *Absolutely*, she wanted to say, but instead she just said yes, a word that now seemed tender instead of weak.

As the days passed and then flew by, Suzette felt more beautiful than she had in years. Even Mig noticed. "Did you do something to your hair?" he asked one day.

"Nope."

"You sure?"

"Did you sign the permission slip for Lena's field trip?" Suzette asked.

"Sorry," Mig said. "I forgot." Again.

"This one's out of town, so she needs both our signatures."

"I know, I know," Mig said. "I got it. I'll turn it in tomorrow."

Lonnie was a chemist, but Suzette thought of him as her alchemist: he was transforming her days into gold. Suzette especially liked that he gushed over every single thing she baked: apricot rugelach filled with jam and nuts and raisins, as well as baklava, honey-soaked and flaky. He claimed each item was marvelous, outstanding, incredible.

And his hands—Lonnie's hands smelled unbelievably like marzipan. She suspected he used almond soap or lotion but never found evidence of either the two times he invited her to his house, when Naomi was spending the night at Lindy's. His hands had to be touching her face for her to catch the scent. How could a man smell like something as divine as marzipan, a candy that wasn't readily available, that you had to seek out, that once you tried, you loved?

One night, their ninth date, Lonnie surprised Suzette by taking her to see *The Godfather* on the Best of the '70s Night at the theater. *The Godfather* had been Mig's favorite movie.

"Have you seen it before?" Lonnie asked while they waited in line for popcorn.

"Uh-huh."

"It's a classic. Did you like it?" Lonnie's hair was longer now than it had been in early fall. It fell in his eyes sometimes, and he pushed it out of his face.

"It was okay," Suzette said.

"You didn't like it."

"I didn't say that." Suzette pretended to be focused on the boxes of candy in the case.

"Look, we don't need to stay for this. Let's do something else."

"You already bought the tickets," Suzette said. "We're here."

"So what?"

"You want to see this movie."

"Not if you don't."

"It's been a long time, that's all," she said. "It'll be good for me to see it again. I was so young the first time."

"You sure?" He was already smiling.

She could do this, couldn't she? It was one tiny thing. How hard could one movie be? "Positive," she said.

"Did you want some candy?"

"The popcorn is enough."

Early on, Suzette knew she was in trouble. The movie started, and her throat tightened. Lonnie held her hand, and she hoped he wasn't aware that hers was sweating. She let go of his for a moment and wiped her hand on her jeans. Lonnie was so absorbed in the movie he didn't seem to notice.

"This is one of my favorite scenes," he sometimes whispered, or, "Can you believe this writing? Incredible."

Suzette wanted to cry throughout all of it but held in her emotions until the end when Michael lied and assured Kay that he had played no part in Carlo's death. Suzette's tears weren't because Mig had ever lied to her; they were because she could see the characters' marital seams beginning to tear apart at a time when they still had a chance to stop it. Suzette got up, pushed past the other seated patrons—"Sorry, sorry"—and hurried to the bathroom. She clicked the stall shut and cried as silently as possible, a trick she had learned when she was a kid.

She met Lonnie afterward out in the lobby.

"You okay?" he asked.

"I just needed some water. All that popcorn made me thirsty."

Long ago she had found that a little truth could be stretched to look like a whole one.

The first time Lonnie mistakenly called Suzette "Lindy" (they were in his kitchen, washing and drying dishes, and he asked her, "Lindy, can you hand me that?") Suzette laughed it off. The second time (this one on the phone right after he said, "I miss you") Suzette treated it as one does a fart that uncontrollably squeezes out: she ignored it. And the third time, which happened at Lonnie's house, the moment after he had so skillfully unhooked and removed her bra, Suzette thought of the tick-tick-ticking sound of a bomb, and she rose from his bed, grabbed her bra and balled it up in her hand as if she were going to lob it, and walked out of Lonnie's house without saying a word, not because she was angry but because it seemed easier than an uncomfortable conversation, and she was tired of conversation. Her whole life felt like it had been one uncomfortable conversation.

The last time Suzette saw Lonnie Newman was at a PTA meeting, two days later. He did not speak to her, and she did not speak to him. As parents settled into the chairs around the circle, she felt his eyes on her, but she refused to turn his way. If he wanted to have a word with her, all he had to do was come up and say something. Surely he would.

Miss DeWitt introduced the newest parent and handed out a fresh parent roster on pink paper filled with M's and D's and S's, and there was a contentious conversation about whether to sell candy that had peanuts in it at the holiday concert. When it was over, the parents rushed to leave, as did Lonnie. Suzette was the last one, and she tossed her parent roster, the one with the D by her name, into the trash can as she left.

He did not show up at the next PTA meeting or the next, and Suzette found she was not mad at his disappearance or at the fact that he was still grieving his breakup—it made it easier to believe that she was not. She drove home, her headlights cutting through the solid night.

"How was PTA?" Mig asked when she walked in her front door. He was leaning against the kitchen counter, checking out his new phone.

"Where's Lena?"

"She was upstairs reading, but I'm pretty sure she's fallen asleep."

"I guess that's good." But was it? It was only 7:30. Was Lena that tired? Was she as tired as Suzette? She set her bag on the counter. "I'm buying a house," Suzette said.

"You're what?"

"My mom gave me some of my inheritance early, and I'm gonna do it—sell this place and find a home for me and Lena." Suzette kicked off her shoes.

"Wow," Mig said. He jammed the phone into his pocket.

The floor creaked as Suzette moved toward the kitchen table. "I downloaded all the For Sale by Owner papers," she said. "Is that still how you want to do it?"

"I guess, I mean, how hard can it be?"

"You're on your own with it, like I told you before." Suzette unbuttoned her coat, pulled it off, and hung it on the back of a kitchen chair. "Just give me a heads up if you have a showing so I can get out of here. Do you need help with the paperwork? The website has instructions."

"No, I got it."

"Great," she said. Her stomach rumbled, but she wasn't sure if she felt hungry anymore. "You can finally get your money out of this place."

"Yeah," Mig said. He took his phone out again but did not look at it, just turned it over and over in his palm.

The yellow walls of the kitchen felt too bright. Suzette's eyes ached.

"Well, I'm happy for you," Mig said, glancing toward the kitchen window. "Good for you."

"Yep," Suzette said, putting a hand on her stomach to quiet it. "Good for me."

LUNGS OF WINTER

Sometimes Suzette wished she could go back in time—not to change things, as some people wanted, not to undo decisions made, but to enjoy the good more. She had spent most of her adult life fretting over the bad things that might happen, and this had threatened to eclipse so many of the better things, like her and Mig's honeymoon. They had driven across the country and back. This had been Mig's idea, of course. They had just graduated with master's degrees (he in philosophy, she in counseling) and Mig had said, "It's our last summer of freedom. Time to hit the road." Suzette hesitated but gave in, as she often did with Mig. Sometimes it was easier than contradicting him, but oftentimes, too—in fact nearly all the time—giving in opened a door. On their honeymoon, they had eaten at greasy diners and truck stops, sweated through their shirts while hiking in more than a dozen national parks, crossed the paths of two rattlesnakes, chased off raccoons, and heated up baked beans and cooked corn bread over fires.

Suzette had enjoyed it enough at the time, but now, in hindsight, so many years later, which was so often the case with her, she wished she had relished it more, had not worried so much about where they would sleep, how hard it might rain, whether Mig's old station wagon would make it. That summer, for the first time, Suzette did not wear a watch—Mig had made that suggestion—and they lived by the light of each day, awakening at dawn and drifting off to sleep as stars burned the sky. They camped mostly or slept in the back of the beat-up wagon that seemed to hold up through deserts and on gravel roads and across whatever terrain Mig decided to traverse. Mig knew how to change everything from oil to belts and hoses, and he could fashion temporary fixes out of common items: metal hangers, paper clips, plastic water bottles. Mig had a way with things he loved, instinctively knowing how to do just enough to make them last. He had done that with their marriage, too, until he'd run out of things to do, or run out of love. Or, perhaps, both.

Mig's call punctured Suzette's workday the way a pin does a balloon.

"It's a long drive from New York," Suzette said, leaning toward her office phone to talk via speaker to her ex-husband of four years. Mig was proposing to drive their daughter back to North Carolina on Saturday instead of putting her on the plane on Sunday as planned.

"I know how long the drive is," he said.

"It's not pretty here in November, you know," Suzette said. Through the window, ripe red leaves fluttered from the maple, the last of the trees to give up their foliage. "Everything has already fallen."

"Since when do I drive to see leaves?" Mig asked. "And anyway, everything has fallen here, too."

"What does Lena think of the idea?"

"You kidding me? A road trip? Donuts, Fritos, Pepsi and—"

"Mig."

"I'm joking. I told her we'd stop in DC and see a couple of monuments. She's all about it."

Suzette's office felt drafty, and she reached down to plug in the space heater at her feet.

"You used to want me to drive Lena here and back, and now that I'm doing it . . . what gives? You got a date or something, Suze?" Mig hadn't called her "Suze" since the early years of their marriage, which seemed an awfully long time ago. Maybe because it was. "Cancel it," Mig said. "We'll be way more fun than whatever you've got planned." He was probably right, but it was too late to change her plans. Suzette's cousin Nathaniel and his wife—both of whom Suzette hadn't seen in years—were driving through the Triangle on their way to the coast and had invited Suzette out for dinner.

Outside, white clouds suffocated the sun. "Have you cancelled her plane ticket already?" she asked Mig.

"Yep."

"Then there's no use talking about it, is there." Goodness, she sounded just like her mother. "Look, Mig, I have to run. Flavia and I have a meeting." Flavia was indeed standing in Suzette's office doorway holding a stuffed manila folder, her black hair in a high bun, which meant she was ready to organize, plan, and rule. She was scrunching up her nose at the sound of Mig's voice.

"Hi, Flavia," he said loudly.

"Mig," Flavia answered with a shake of her head. As soon as Suzette hung up, Flavia asked, "Why is he driving Lena?"

The space heater kicked on with a rattle. "He always did like driving."

"But to here? He hates this place."

"I stopped trying to figure him out a long time ago."

"Where's he going to stay?"

Probably Suzette's house. "I forgot to ask," Suzette said, rubbing her forehead, which had just begun to hurt. The heater whirred and warmed her feet.

Mig had finally moved to New York City three years ago—well, New Jersey, really, but Mig called it all New York City because he was so desperate to be there instead of Chapel Hill. He had always claimed there was no other "real" place to live, to which Suzette had finally said, "What do you think—everywhere else is imaginary? Are Lena and I imaginary, too?" It embarrassed Suzette, this aberrant outburst, one of several during the first year of their divorce, and she had apologized twice before Mig said, "Quit saying you're sorry for how you really feel."

Because of Lena, Suzette had protested Mig's moving back up north until it finally occurred to her that it would be better for their daughter if Mig were happier, something Mig wasn't good at to begin with. With Suzette's tepid blessing, he had left and moved into his uncle's basement in Jersey City until he saved enough to rent a studio apartment. Suzette worried about Lena having no bedroom when she visited him, but Lena, even now at ten years old, thought of each visit as an adventure. Lena had become a little expert at packing her own suitcase and learning the routines of flight attendants accompanying her from her mother's hand to her father's. All this made Lena comfortable on planes, able to sleep on any leg, no matter the volume of the engine, no matter how short the flight. Suzette could never sleep on any plane, and she marveled at how easily Lena shuttled back and forth one long weekend every month of the school year, rising early on flight mornings, eager to get to the airport, regardless of the fact that when at Mig's she slept on a blow-up bed, ate on paper plates, drank from plastic cups, and had to shower in lukewarm water and jiggle the toilet handle after each flush. Lena loved it all.

And Mig, well, he had become easier since leaving, less irritable and argumentative, especially in the last six months, probably because he could breathe the air of freedom. She and Mig had not seen each other for a while, had instead learned to negotiate Lena's schedule by phone and email. Suzette was sure that Mig's girlfriends also had a direct impact on his elevated mood. Lena mentioned these girlfriends now and again, without Suzette's prompting: Regina, who wore tube tops and short skirts and who squeaked when she talked, according to Lena; Electra, who used "bad words she should not be using" and who owned only one pair of shoes, or at least that was all Lena ever saw her in—thigh-high black leather boots, which Lena for a time wanted, much to Suzette's horror. Lena said Electra had "big boobs" and called Mig "Daddy-O," which prompted Suzette to ask how old Electra was. Lena answered, "Maybe sixteen?" Suzette had to work up the nerve for weeks to ask Mig, who laughed and laughed before assuring Suzette that Electra was in fact thirty-nine. Then they had both laughed, which was the first time that had happened since the divorce.

Recently, Lena told Suzette that Mig had lost a lot of weight and had accidentally mentioned someone named Roan.

"What do you mean 'accidentally'?"

"I asked who Roan was," Lena said, "and he pretended he had to go pee. She must be a secret. Do you think she's married?"

This was exactly why Suzette thought of Lena as only ten-year-old*ish*. "I don't know, baby, but don't worry, okay?"

"I'm not worried. Her being married would be cool."

Dear God. Suzette wasn't sure if it was better for Roan to be single or married. There was the morality of it all and what it was teaching her daughter. On the other hand, if Roan was still married, she couldn't become Lena's stepmother, at least not until Roan's divorce was final, and that would take a while, wouldn't it? Maybe Lena would be in high school by then, or better yet, college. Or how about never? What if Lena thought being with someone who was married was a great thing even when she became an adult? What if that was all she strived for?

Suzette hoped if Roan was a secret, Mig would keep it that way, but she had a feeling coiling in the pit of her stomach about this unnecessary trip he was making to North Carolina. She breathed deeply, in and out, in and out, doing her best to blow the cloud of worry from this Mig-marbled sky.

Suzette risked being late for the PTA meeting by going home after work first, but she wanted to grab something to eat before sitting through what often turned into a tedious discussion. She entered her neighborhood, one she had picked after the divorce for its wide sidewalks, its crape myrtles that stood like a row of blooming watchmen along the streets in summer, and the roundabouts and cul-de-sacs where Lena roller-skated, where cars slowed for kids, and where Lena could leave her blue bike lying on its side overnight and always find it again.

As Suzette pulled into her driveway, she noticed a box on her front stoop. Darkness had fallen already—November was notorious for shutting down its days too soon—but the streetlight gave off enough glow for Suzette to discern the package. She hadn't ordered anything. Could it be something from Mig? In the last few months, he had not only been mailing her articles, mostly newspaper or magazine clippings of things he guessed (correctly) might interest her—a Gloria Steinem profile, a review of a Jane Austen film—but on her birthday three and a half weeks ago, Mig had sent her a padded envelope stuffed with bars of dark chocolate and a set of magnets with Tiffany stained glass designs. Mig had never been much of a gift-giver. When they were married, it had been his idea, before they had Lena, not to exchange Christmas gifts at all. And although for every one of those Christmases Suzette had been unable to resist secretly buying him at least a small something—a pair of winter gloves or a Nirvana CD—he had never secretly bought her anything.

His recent birthday gift to Suzette had made her wonder what it was he hoped she would give up in the exchange. More time with Lena? More weeks out of the coming summer? He had cancelled a bunch of weeks this past one, last minute, probably because of Roan. And while Suzette had not wanted to love the gift, she had, though she did not admit this to him. If nothing else, their marriage had taught her to downplay feelings. Or maybe she had learned that from her mother, who always said it was better to be strong than sensitive. At any rate, Suzette merely said thank you to Mig and that the gift was thoughtful, two sentences that did not merit the time she had spent thinking of them and that she dropped into the end of a phone conversation with Mig about logistics concerning Lena. Before Mig could respond, Suzette rushed off the call. She didn't tell anyone about Mig's birthday gift, not even Flavia, who would have asked more questions for which Suzette had no answers. How could she know what Mig was thinking? And no, she did not want to ask him.

Now, as she walked toward the package on her stoop, she wondered what Mig might have sent that would be this big. *Too big* from the looks of it. If it contained something expensive—had Lena told him about the set of purple plates Suzette had been eyeing from Bennington Potters?—she would have to refuse them. Oh, but Suzette loved those plates. And they would be worth it. Hadn't her mother always told her to purchase only things that cost enough to last a lifetime? Perhaps Suzette could tell Mig that she would pay him for them. Yes, she could do that, and then that would put an end to this whole gift-giving thing, whatever it meant (all of next summer with Lena since he had seen his daughter so seldom this past one?).

Suzette lifted the box—heavy enough to contain at least four dinner plates—and wrestled with the house key and door and fumbled with the light switch in the living room. That's when she saw: the return address was not Mig's but her mother's. Suzette should have guessed this since her mother had mentioned she was "purging" another room in the house. Whenever this happened, Suzette received a package of some ancient artifact from her childhood that her sentimental father had held on to and that her mother now wanted to throw away but instead relinquished to Suzette so she could toss it out herself. Suzette hated these packages because they always carried memories, and memories inherently contained not just stories but absences, reminders of all that had been lost since then.

With a kitchen knife, Suzette sliced the tape and lifted the edges of the package. Inside, no note, just crumpled brown paper wrapped around something smelling of leather polish. Suzette didn't have to unfold the paper to know what the box contained, so she didn't. It was a pair of old red ice skates. And because she had no need to view them, Suzette closed the box and toted it out to the car, plopping it into the trunk before heading to PTA. It wasn't until she was almost there that her stomach growled. Suzette had forgotten to grab something to eat, and now, as was true with so many things, it was entirely too late.

In her youth, Suzette had shone in many things: playing flute, mastering algebra, French braiding her own hair, reading her mother's moods by how quickly she stirred her coffee, and keeping silent, even receding when necessary. Suzette could fix the cassette player when it chewed up tapes; she knew how much to water and prune her mother's finicky rose bushes; and she could bake a divine, crumbly yet soft, Russian tea cake. But back then, she excelled the most at figure skating, not because she possessed greater skill in it but because she felt more alive on the ice than anywhere else. Her father was the one who suggested she take lessons when she was eleven, and her mother responded, "Well if you want to take her, go right ahead." He hurried home from work on Tuesdays and Thursdays and drove Suzette the forty minutes through Buffalo traffic so she could learn to fly.

This is how she thought of it now that she was in her forties: for six beautiful years, her father had given her the gift of flight. He had bought Suzette her first pair of skates (pink ones with pink laces) and her last pair (red skates, white laces). He had sat on the benches outside the rink, plexiglass between them, and watched his daughter whirl around the ice, cold burnishing her face as she learned the toe loop jump and the half lutz and let her light and lean body whip the air as if it could not be troubled with pausing.

And then when Suzette was seventeen, her father began to cough. He coughed and coughed and sucked on cherry lozenges and kept handkerchiefs tucked in his pockets. He drank orange juice at every meal and drank hot tea with honey before bed, until a doctor held up an X-ray showing white spots on black lungs. Suzette's father had never once smoked, and this seemed the most egregious to Suzette: that something bad could happen to someone so good while he hadn't been looking, while he was doing nothing wrong.

Though she had her driver's license by then, and her mother might have loaned her the Chevy Impala on Tuesdays and Thursdays if her father had pleaded enough on her behalf, Suzette quit skating. Her father tried to talk her out of it, but her mother, for once, seemed to understand and told him the decision was made.

Suzette told her father she did not love skating anymore, but that
wasn't true; it was just the closest to the truth she could get at seventeen.
It was only years later, after her father died, that Suzette realized she
had stopped skating not because she did not love the sport but because
it no longer felt good to love anything or anyone. It no longer seemed
fair to feel alive.

Suzette arrived late to the PTA meeting, which she hated doing. She
tried entering the room quietly, slipping into the seat closest to the
door, but Ms. Reynolds, strict about punctuality, glared in her direction.
Only after Suzette shook off her jacket did she glance around the room.
She thought for a moment she was seeing things, but no, it was him:
Lonnie Newman, after all these years, across the way. He smiled at her.

Suzette fidgeted in her seat. Someone—some mother—had doused
her whole body in perfume, and it permeated the air as if it were planting itself into Suzette's pores. Her nose itched, but she did not reach to
scratch it. On the chalkboard, Ms. Reynolds had scrawled someone's
quote, "We're all in this together. They are all our kids," but this made
Suzette think of the Lily Tomlin quote, "We are all in this together, by
ourselves." Suzette tried to focus on what Ms. Reynolds was saying
about the revised budget for soccer team jerseys, but Lena didn't play
soccer, and there was Lonnie Newman. How about that. Lonnie, the
only man she had really dated since she and Mig had split. She had
nearly forgotten about him, or perhaps just tried her best to. Sometimes
it was hard to tell the difference.

When the PTA meeting concluded, Suzette remained in her chair,
rummaging in her purse for nothing. The last thing she wanted to do
was exit the meeting at the same time as Lonnie and end up in the
hallway together.

"Hey," Lonnie said, appearing next to her chair. "I didn't know if
you'd be here." Had he been hoping she would or wouldn't? "How've
you been?" He extended his hand.

She took it, lifting herself up with his grip, and stood facing him.
"The same." Those gray eyes, looking so much like smoke. She'd
nearly forgotten them.

"I heard you and Flavia are running The Women's Center now.
Congratulations."

Taking over the nonprofit had been challenging with a persnickety
board, grants that had brought in less, fundraising that demanded more,

but she and Flavia, together, had managed. They'd even succeeded in hauling the center from near-shutdown.

"You heard that?" she asked.

"I kept up with you." Lonnie smiled shyly. "I always kept up, even when I was in Texas."

"Texas?"

He smiled again, but this time the corners of his mouth did not rise. "I guess you haven't kept up with me."

"I'm sorry, I—"

"No, I get it. You had no reason to. That's my fault. Anyway, I've been in Texas the last two and a half years. I got transferred there to help start a new lab, but now it's up and running, and I'm back."

"Did you want to come back?"

"I had to negotiate a few things to convince those at the top that it would be better if I were here, but I never doubted it'd be worth it."

"Your daughter, of course."

"Yes, my daughter, but other things, too." He tilted his head. Her stomach fluttered. "How are you, Suzette?" he asked again.

"I'm good, really good." Was she? She felt that way now.

"I'd love to catch up sometime," he said. "Could we do that?"

"Sure." Was this bad? Maybe she should say no. "I just don't know when."

"That's okay," he said. "Well, maybe sometime then."

"Maybe sometime then," she said, her old habit of echoing that her mother used to say made it sound as if Suzette were trapped in a cave.

How did other women seem to know things instantly? Ask her to read the temperature of a board meeting based on how satisfied the members were with program results, ask her to say whether Flavia was feeling generous or anxious on any given day, ask her even what kind of mood any of her employees was in when they walked in the door, and Suzette could tell with such accuracy it might as well have flashed digital. Ask her about her own feelings? Not her forte. Ask her what was best for Lena, or Flavia, or even her mother, and Suzette supplied an instant answer, quicker than the next person could crack open a fortune cookie. But when it came to what she wanted for herself, Suzette's wishes were sunk deep into an ocean of shoulds, second guesses, and fears.

As for predicting the future, Suzette might as well have played the lottery with her guesses. Flavia said the first time she met her husband,

Patrick, she knew he was the one. They were both volunteering at the state fair, pouring funnel cake batter into the fryer, when he burned his hand pretty badly from the grease. He never so much as cursed, simply shrugged it off, and that's the moment she knew she wanted to marry him. Perhaps Flavia had developed this perception over time and experience: she had confided to Suzette that when she was younger she had been in love with someone else for years after their official breakup. It had taken Flavia a long time to truly move on, and when she did, she met Patrick, and she just knew. Now they had six-year-old twins, Daisy and Marigold. Flavia had known she was pregnant with them the day after they'd been conceived. She'd also known she was having multiples before the ultrasound. How? "It just felt like a crowd in there," she said.

All of this baffled Suzette, who could not guess at any one thing, even if it walked naked in front of her and did a little jig.

When Mig and Lena arrived, they tumbled out of the car in laughter. Suzette peeked out from behind the curtain of the living room window. She had been waiting there for twenty minutes. This was something she used to do when they were all still a family—watch them when they didn't know she was. Mig would have probably called her too sentimental.

She opened the front door and stepped out.

"Suze!" Mig waved. When did Mig start waving? He was indeed a lot thinner than before; his flannel shirt flopped around him. And his hair, usually shaggy, was close-shaven. "Come look at this," he said.

Lena was cradling something in the palm of her hand. She held it out for Suzette: a tiny turtle, three inches long.

"Don't worry," he said. "She's not going to keep it. We saw it when we made a pit stop. It was gonna get run over. I let her take it as long as she promised to set it free when we got here."

"I can put it near our creek, right, Dad?"

"Sure. If that's okay with you?" he asked Suzette.

"Of course," she said. "Can you let your dad hold that for a sec?" Once Lena surrendered the turtle, Suzette drew Lena into her arms and held her close, taking in her daughter's lemony scent. "I missed you," Suzette said. "I have to get going, but I'll be back."

"Now?" Mig said. "Really? You should have cancelled."

"I'm not the cancelling type."

"It's not a date, is it?"

Why did he always think she wasn't dating? Not that she had in years, but still. "Who wants to know?"

"I do!" Lena said.

"I'm meeting your Uncle Nathaniel and Aunt Maggie," Suzette said to Lena, running her hands through her daughter's silky hair.

Lena's face fell. "Oh."

Suzette and Mig laughed. Their eyes met, and Suzette stopped laughing. "I've gotta run," she said.

"Would it be alright if I crashed here?" Mig asked.

Surprise, surprise. She had in fact changed the guest bed sheets last night. "Did you pack your cooking skills in your bag?" she asked.

"Suze, c'mon. It's me. I'm still the culinary master." He had been, but only when he felt like it, which was almost never. He was more like the Master of Snacks.

"Then feed Lena something good, and save some for me since I know I won't be eating much there. They wanted to meet at a bar, of all places."

"You got it," Mig said. "What'll it be?" he asked Lena. "Green bean stew? Raw eggplant with paprika? Zucchini on a stick?"

"Gross," Lena said.

"Go on," Mig said to Suzette. "We'll be here."

After she got in the car, she lingered for a moment in the driveway, watching the two of them stand opposite each other, Mig leaning down to inspect the teeny turtle in Lena's palm and then saying something that made Lena smile, something Suzette would of course never hear. The evening broke open, as if from silence to sound, like a song she had forgotten for years and just remembered.

From the half-circle booth across the room, Maggie waved like a referee at Suzette. "Hey, over here!" Which made Suzette blush.

"Howdy," Nathaniel said, rising as Suzette approached. He kissed her on the cheek.

Nathaniel was reedy, just like Suzette, just like everyone in their family, and Maggie, though petite, always struck Suzette as ready to throw a football in your face.

"You look great," Maggie said, grinning. Scattered across the table were several empty and half-full glasses of who-knows-what.

"It's good to see you all," Suzette said. "It's been too long." It had not been too long. Why did she automatically say such things? She loved Nathaniel but could only tolerate Maggie in small doses. "How many years has it been?"

"Can't remember," Nathaniel said.

"Oh, I remember," Maggie said. "We saw you at your Uncle Paul's funeral."

"Yes, right." Suzette squeezed into the booth with them, Maggie in the middle.

"You looked awful," Maggie said.

"I did?"

"God, yes. You and Mig were . . . in the final stages." Like a disease.

"I suppose so. Is this one mine?"

Maggie slid a glass to her. The water shook inside. "I don't think I've ever seen you look so bad, and sure, we all have our bad days, but not like that." Maggie poked Nathaniel with her elbow. "Don't you agree, honey?"

"You look great now," he said to Suzette.

"You do," Maggie said. "Stunning, in fact."

"Thank you."

"What kind of color do you use in your hair to cover the gray?" Maggie squinted at Suzette. "It's fabulous."

"This is my natural color."

"No way."

"I was out in the yard a lot this past summer. The sun bleached it lighter."

"So you used the sun. I knew you'd used something."

Suzette opened a menu. "Have you all already picked out what you want?"

"Don't you love how she says 'y'all'?" Maggie said to Nathaniel. "So southern. It's like we're visiting a foreign country."

Suzette wanted to say that it felt like they were foreigners, too. Nathaniel offered an apologetic smile to Suzette.

"I was surprised you didn't bring the kids," Suzette said.

"Not on this one," Maggie said. "This is *our* special trip."

"Oh?"

"Natty, you didn't tell her?"

"What is it?" Suzette asked.

"We have news," Nathaniel said in a low voice, leaning conspiratorially toward Suzette. He put his arm around Maggie, who giggled.

Suzette was going to ask if Maggie was pregnant, but she thought better of it. "You want another kid?" she asked.

"No, no, no," Maggie said. "Three's enough."

"Then?"

"We just got married!" Maggie said. "Two days ago!" She held out her hand so Suzette could admire her fat diamond ring.

"It's beautiful, but you were already married."

"Yes, but again," Maggie said. "We renewed our vows, and we want to thank you for it."

"Me?"

"It was because of seeing your marriage blow up that we began to work on ours. The last thing we wanted was to go through what you went through." Maggie beamed.

"I don't know what to say. You're welcome?"

"Let's celebrate. Want to make a toast?" Nathaniel raised his glass, and Maggie did, too. Suzette reluctantly raised her water glass.

"To marriage!" Maggie said.

"I'm not married," Suzette said.

"Yes, but one day you will be again," Nathaniel said.

"Yes, she will!" Maggie took a gulp from her glass without clinking it against anyone else's. Nathaniel clinked his glass with Suzette's.

"They all recycle eventually," Maggie said. "Except my Natty here." She kissed him on the cheek and giggled again. "Now if you'll excuse me, I need to go use the powder room. Too many drinks makes a girl need to pee-pee." Suzette slid out and waited while Maggie scooted from the booth. "Don't tell secrets while I'm gone, okay? Shhhhhhh." She teetered away, holding onto the back of a booth now and again to keep her balance, waving at customers in other booths as she passed them.

As soon as she was out of sight, Suzette said, "Oh my," as she slid back into the booth.

"I'm sorry, Suzette." Nathaniel said. "She's just tipsy. Well, probably more than tipsy."

"I sure hope so. Are you?"

"I wish."

"Maggie said this was your honeymoon."

"She's not telling you everything." Nathaniel slumped back against the booth.

A waiter came by. "Are you ready to order?"

"My wife wants some fries."

"Regular fries or sweet potato?" the waiter asked Suzette.

"I'm not the wife," she said.

"Oh. My apologies."

"Regular," Nathaniel said. "She likes everything regular."

"And for you, ma'am?"

"I don't think I'm going to have anything just yet." Suzette's appetite had teetered away, too.

"Should I leave the menus?" the waiter asked.

"She had an affair," Nathaniel said to Suzette.

"She what? No."

"I'm just going leave the menus," the waiter said.

"It was my fault, really." Nathaniel ran his finger around the rim of his glass, which was about an inch from being empty of something on the rocks. Suzette half expected the glass to start whistling, but Nathaniel had never had the kind of talent that made anything sing. "I was neglectful," he said. "She slept with one of our neighbors, someone she didn't even find all that attractive, really, but, I guess when you're desperate . . ."

"I'm so sorry, Nathaniel."

"Don't be. He drank Five Alive and loved Harry Potter. He had a Hogwarts acceptance letter framed in his living room."

"So you were friends?"

"He and his wife had us over once when they first moved in. Then they got divorced, and, well, I guess he was lonely, and so was Maggie." Nathaniel reached for his napkin and spread it open on the table. "Anyway, he moved just after I found out. The affair was brief, only a few months." He folded the napkin into smaller and smaller triangles. "I think she wanted me to figure out on my own—looking back, I realize she left a ton of clues—but I just never in a billion years thought to suspect."

"I understand that."

"She eventually had to tell me or else I never would have known. What can I say?" The napkin was now tiny and tight and neat. "It was tough, but if all that awful stuff hadn't happened, we wouldn't be where we are today, you know? We're good."

"Are you?"

"I think so," he said. "We just got married, so I hope so."

"I don't know what to say."

"Can't blame you." Nathaniel wiped some condensation from the outside of his glass with the triangle.

"Is this really what you want?" Suzette asked.

"It's what I have," he said, and he drank what was left in his glass and set it down, the ice clattering around the bottom.

On the drive home, ZZ's Ice Arena rose up ahead, a giant box of a building that could block any good view. Suzette rarely drove this route, and when she did, she did not pay attention to the arena. Now she slowed down. The parking lot was overflowing with cars, and several sets of parents were tugging their kids in and out of the hulking building. Suzette sped up again, switching on the radio, searching for a tune she liked.

When she arrived home, a sweet aroma flirted from the kitchen.

"Hey, Suze," Mig said when she swung open the kitchen door. He was holding a spatula even though he was seated at the kitchen table. "We made pancakes." When they were married, Mig had made these for dinner, and although eating pancakes for dinner did not meet any of her qualifications for nutrition, his pancakes, pillowy and moist, always tasted better than any healthful meal she could think of.

Mig handed a plate to Suzette, and she picked up the bottle of maple syrup on the table, drizzling some all over the pancake on top and then taking one glorious bite.

"The syrup is the kind you like, Canadian Finest," Lena said. "Dad picked it out."

"He did?" Lena and Mig were both watching her intently. Suzette finished chewing and swallowed. "Thank you," she said, unsure what else she was supposed to say. "What is it?"

"What's what?" Mig asked.

"Did something happen while I was out?"

"Nope, we just set the turtle free." Mig stood and started clearing dishes, rinsing them in the sink. "How's ol' Natty?"

"Nathaniel's fine. On his way to happiness, I think."

"About time." When they were still married, Mig and Suzette had had plenty of discussions about how unhappy Nathaniel seemed. "Always knew he had it in him," Mig said. "Can take a man a while to figure out, but we get there."

She nodded, thinking of how Mig had finally made it back north. She thought of Roan and pushed the thought away. Suzette wanted more butter between the top and bottom pancake. She dug into the butter tub with her knife, lifting a big and delicious glob. Oh, she shouldn't be doing this—it was too much. Suzette put back some of it. Then she put back all of it, pressing the knife along the tub's side. No, she was allowed something. She dug again and dabbed a pat of butter between the two pancakes and resumed eating.

Mig put his hands on their daughter's shoulders. "Sweetie, why don't you go watch some TV in the other room?"

"Can I take some pancakes?"

"Have at it."

Suzette laid down her fork and wiped her hands with a paper towel as Lena walked out with a plate of stacked pancakes she could never finish on her own, but Suzette didn't say a word. Lena, in her pink T-shirt and PJ bottoms with hearts, disappeared through the swinging door, and Suzette thought, *nothing good ever lasts long enough,* something her mother might have said. Suzette stabbed a big chunk of pancake and stuffed it in her mouth.

"We need to talk," Mig said. These had always been Suzette's words, the ones she used to present bad news when they were still together. Now she understood why his shoulders had slumped every time.

"What is it, Mig?"

"It's about me." He sat down at the table, *their* old kitchen table. Before they'd had Lena, she and Mig had sanded its golden oak top and stained it one Saturday afternoon.

Mig put his hands on his thighs and leaned forward as if he were going to lecture her. "It's about you, too," he said, "but not in the same way."

"Just spit it out, Mig." Suzette had become less polite with him when under stress. She felt only a little bad about it.

"I'm trying. This isn't easy—not that it's all bad. In fact—"

"What is it." Not a question. She was done with questions.

"Do you remember last summer when I had to cancel some of Lena's trips?"

He had cancelled nearly all of them. She hadn't minded having Lena more, but she didn't like last-minute changes to the schedule. "Of course."

"Well, I never told you why, and you never asked."

"Was I supposed to? I know how you like your privacy."

"I was actually glad you didn't. There was so much happening and changing."

Suzette stood and carried her plate to the sink. She turned on the faucet. The water gurgled then gushed out, splattering the plate. Here is where he would tell her about his soon-to-be wife. She held her plate under the rushing water and let it take all the pancakes with one swish off the plate.

"I was getting cancer treatments," he said.

She swung around. "What?" Water dripped off the plate still in her hand.

"I was diagnosed in early May with colon cancer."

She set the plate in the sink and turned off the faucet. She picked up the scrubber and scoured the face of the plate.

"Suzette?"

She could taste bile.

"Can you please turn around and look at me?"

She did but kept her focus high, on the wall behind him. The wall was the pale blue of a baby pool, a place where no one was supposed to drown. She dropped her gaze to him. He seemed even thinner now, sitting there, clothes drooping. Where was the rest of him? "You waited until now to tell me? That's what—six months?"

"I didn't want to tell you until after the surgery, and the chemotherapy, so I would know what the prognosis was. But then, I needed time to, you know, process it all first, and other things. It's turned my world upside down."

"Does Lena know?"

"No, no, not yet. I mean, she knows I've been sick, but not anything serious. I thought we should tell her together."

"Are you okay now?"

"I have my hair. That's a win, right?"

"Mig, what are the doctors saying?"

"I'm fine. I mean, they think I will be. They got it all."

"You should have prefaced with that."

"I'm sorry. I'm nervous." Mig had never once been nervous in all the years she had known him. Had he? If so, he had never admitted it. "I didn't know how much it would shift everything," he said.

"You should have told me."

"Suzette, I'm sorry."

"You're not that sorry." She stalked out of the kitchen and had to walk, unfortunately, through the living room to get to the stairs.

"Mom?" The plate of mounded pancakes was nestled on Lena's lap.

"Hey, baby." Suzette did not pause or slow down. She went right up the staircase, gripping the banister. She shut her bedroom door and sat on the bed. The mattress was firm and did not give much with her light weight, and for the first time Suzette wondered if Mig had been right when he had insisted a softer bed made for a better sleep, a better everything.

On her dresser lay two stacks of laundry, folded already but not yet put away. Suzette pulled open a drawer and tucked the shirts into their proper place, and then her underwear and socks, but the sock drawer seemed chaotic—not all the socks were folded well—and maybe the athletic socks should be more separated from her work socks, so she grabbed them and dumped them on the bed, the whole lot of them in handfuls, and then she sat on the bed again and grouped them by occasion and then season and sorted the work socks by color, light to dark, like a rainbow drained of color, left with only hues of gray.

There was a knock at the door. "Suze?"

"I'll be downstairs in a minute." Or more.

"Wanna let me in?"

"No," she said.

Mig's steps faded away.

She examined the socks for places they were too worn and started a get-rid-of pile. The bedroom was cool and quiet, offering its solace. The get-rid-of pile got bigger, every sock thinning and threatening holes. Suzette finished sorting, and once all the socks, at least the ones she was keeping, lay back in the sock drawer, folded into pairs, she ambled downstairs to the kitchen, not wanting to go, but the thought of Lena, as usual, propelled her forward.

Mig was washing dishes. Suzette stood just inside the door, not wanting to go farther in, not sure where to go, unrooted and exhausted. "So is that it?" she asked. "Is that all you have to tell me?"

He dried his hands with the yellow dish towel and leaned back against the counter. "Well, no." Clean plates and cups stood upright in the dish rack, but too many more dirty ones still awaited the soapy water—a metal mixing bowl, the oily pan, and Lena hadn't brought in her plate yet. Was Suzette going to have to clean this all up?

She crossed her arms. "Is it more bad news?"

"That was bad but also good news."

"Preface it right this time." She had never talked to him this way in their marriage. Perhaps she should have.

"Suzette, surely you know. If you do, don't make me do this. I don't want to look like a dope."

She steeled herself, ready to hear about maybe-married Roan. "Go ahead and and get it over with."

He laughed. Was he laughing at her?

"Alright," he said. "For you, I will." He set the yellow towel in a bundled lump on the counter. "I think I'm falling in love again. Which might sound preposterous with all that's happened. But it's true. I feel like I finally get it, really get it."

"Are you getting married?"

"What? I don't even know what you think, how you feel. Is that what you want?"

"Do I get a say?" He was *not* getting Lena all of next summer.

"Why are you mad?"

"Because I don't even know a thing about her. Is Roan even married? You left that part out. You're springing all these big things on me. They don't just affect you. They affect me and Lena. Is that why you drove here and made me pancakes, so you could dump a bunch of bad news on me all at once and somehow think that would make it better? Pancakes aren't nearly enough."

"How do you know about Roan?"

"Lena told me you were seeing her."

He rolled his eyes. "I can't get anything past her."

"She's met them all. Why shouldn't she know about this one?"

"All?"

The pancakes, all this ridiculous cooking, had heated the kitchen to stifling. "Yes," Suzette said. "Electra, Roberta, then that one—I can't remember who she was, but she probably had an A-ending name like all the others. She used to smoke with you out on your balcony."

"I quit last year. And Carmela was just a friend," Mig said. "Wait, you think Roan is my girlfriend?"

"Is she married or not? I have a right to know."

Mig started laughing.

"This isn't funny."

"Roan is my therapist."

"You have a physical therapist?"

"My shrink."

"You fell in love with your shrink?"

He laughed again and then stopped when Suzette didn't laugh with him. "Is that really what you think?" His thinness, in such contrast to his former bulky self, reminded Suzette of a plant that suddenly shoots up and grows in early April. Except now it was November.

"I didn't come here just to bring back Lena," Mig said. He stepped toward her. "Suzette, I came back here for you."

The sounds of the television drifted from the living room, canned laughter. The clean dishes glistened in the rack. The oily pan eyed her.

"I'm going out." Suzette grabbed her keys from the golden oak table, the one she had kept all these years, the one he had left behind.

"Now?" Mig asked. "Where?"

"It's past Lena's bedtime."

"Not for another half hour."

"Please put her to bed."

"What's going on?"

"Mig." He of all people should understand. "Please."

"Okay," he said. "Go."

In the parking lot, in the car, engine off, Suzette waited but for what she did not know. The moon was an onion someone had skinned.

She called Flavia, keeping her voice nonchalant, easy, full of nothing. "What are you doing?"

"I've been ironing the girls' dresses for their piano recital tomorrow," Flavia said. "I just found a stain on Daisy's sleeve, but I'm not sure I can get it out. I can't tell if it's food or something disgusting. How about you?"

"I'm at ZZ's Ice Arena."

"What in the world are you doing there?"

"The late-night skate starts at 10:00." At least that's what the flashing sign said. "I think that means no little kids."

"Since when do you skate? Are you okay? Where's Lena? And Mig?"

"They're at home." Her home. Lena's home.

"Did something happen?"

"I just needed some air."

"One of those nights, huh?"

Suzette's ring of keys dangled from the ignition. Bright lights shot from ZZ's glass doors as they swung open and closed and open again, not making up their mind.

"Want to meet me here?" Suzette asked.

"Right now?"

"I know."

"How about we meet up tomorrow after the recital? We'll take you out for an early dinner. Patrick and the girls haven't seen you or Lena in a while. It'll be nice."

"Sure," Suzette said.

"Mig will be gone by then, right?"

"We haven't talked about it." Suzette flicked the ring of keys so that they, too, swung. House, garage, office building, work safe, and what were the rest of these keys for? Why did she carry around all of them?

"He's staying with you, isn't he." An accusation, but a fair one. Flavia was always fair.

Steam climbed across the windows. Suzette rolled down hers; the cool air answered.

"We'll catch up tomorrow, right?" Flavia said. "I want to hear about everything. You sure you're okay?"

"I'm fine. I promise."

Suzette had been fine for a long time now. When she and Mig split, she thought she might not be fine without him, and then she was. With Lonnie she had learned to open her heart, but only enough to let a sliver of light seep through the crack between door and frame, not to let the whole world clamor in. The whole world could glare and scorch. It was easier not to date, not to deal, to just focus on her job and Lena. She was fine. But fine was what you hung on the line to dry, not bothering to bring it in if it rained. Fine was what you drank when you were out of wine and beer and anything else that made you feel good. Fine was the awful smell you couldn't place because it came from everywhere.

Her father would have said do what makes you happy. Her mother would say it doesn't matter what makes you happy; it only matters what is right. Flavia would say try to picture your life five and ten years from now. What do you see in it? Follow the path toward that.

People dawdled in from the parking lot, groups of college-age kids and some young couples in their twenties, laughing and holding hands. Suzette thought back to herself and Mig at that age. Would they have gone skating on a late Friday night? She supposed she would not have wanted to, even then, but she would have gone had Mig suggested it. He would have thought it was silly. Mig had never willingly done anything that might make him look silly or stupid—until, perhaps, now.

Suzette retrieved her old red skates from the box in the trunk, paid her admission, sat on a bench inside, and removed her shoes. The skates' laces were not tied together so that the pair were tethered, the way she might have done for storage, but instead were each tied with a simple knot, and Suzette wondered if she had done that decades ago or if her mother had done this only recently. Suzette's father had known dozens of knot types, and he had taught Suzette a knot that assured the laces would not come undone at a moment's notice, that the two loops hung prettily on each side. But Suzette could not remember how to tie that knot anymore.

The laces slipped apart with one pluck.

Suzette tried to tug the right skate onto her foot, but the skate refused, too tight and small now, ungiving, unable. Skaters whirled around the ice, making it all look so easy. The DJ played '80s pop: the Go-Gos, Pat Benatar, the Commodores. Cold tingled against Suzette's cheeks, her ears, even her hands—she'd left the house without taking anything to protect her from the chill—and she pressed them underneath her legs to warm them. After a few minutes of watching, despite her hesitation, she walked to the rental counter and handed over three dollars. "Size eight and a half, please." A half-size bigger than she had been at seventeen.

She was just finishing lacing them when someone tapped her shoulder.

"Who else is ever going ask me to a late-night skate again?" Flavia's black hair was swept back into a ponytail, a gold hoop glinting in each ear. She was wearing a white down vest, the perfect contrast to her olive skin. She handed Suzette a pair of blue mittens interwoven with strands of sparkling silver thread.

"I owe you for this," Suzette said.

"No, you don't."

When they were both ready—ice skates on, and each wrapped in a fuzzy scarf, hands inside their mittens (Flavia had brought double of everything)—Flavia held out her hand and Suzette took it, and they tottered together to the rink.

Flavia stepped on and moved forward with a few smooth strokes. A natural.

"You're a fantastic skater," Suzette called out from the side.

"My teachers were the long Ohio seasons of freezing," Flavia said as she circled back to Suzette. "You and I, we both grew up with lungs of winter." She stopped in front of Suzette. "Toe pick. You coming out here?"

It had seemed like such a good idea before. Suzette loved this once.

The couples held hands as they floated around the rink. One woman skated backwards, coaxing, pulling a man forward with his stiff, uncertain stride.

"I don't know if I want to anymore," Suzette said.

"You don't have to then."

"But we're here. You're here. You came all the way for this."

"No, I didn't." Flavia stepped off the ice. "I came here for you."

The DJ called out a dedication from Kevin to Lucy, "celebrating three happy months!"

"Three months?" Suzette said. "That's not a milestone. That's like walking out your front door to get the paper."

"We all have to start somewhere."

A Backstreet Boys song came on, and a woman with two long auburn braids whizzed by on the rink. Her face was pink and sweating, like an apple just out of the fridge.

"I don't know what I'm doing," Suzette said.

"It's just ice."

"No, it isn't."

"Yes," Flavia said. "It is."

When Suzette pulled up to her house, she switched off the engine but lingered in the car, the windshield a slanted canvas of the place that had become a home to her and Lena. She thought of the garden beds next to the front stoop where the mulch was dwindling, as it always did this time of year. She thought of how the house needed painting, but no one could tell except Suzette, who always noticed the spots where it was peeling. Now, in the semidarkness, except for the light hovering over the front door and of course the streetlight that cast its perpetual glow, you couldn't tell the house wanted for anything. Its color, dark gray, the color of contemplation, blended into the night, and the house rose two stories, sure of its stature, appearing perfectly capable of all the comfort in the world, all that she needed. Suzette thought of the left gutter that needed mucking out. She would do that next weekend, Lena holding the ladder at the bottom.

Lena's two windows lay empty and motionless, curtains drawn. So he'd put her to bed. Good.

Suzette's phone beeped, alerting her to a text. Lonnie Newman. So he'd kept her number all these years. Well, she'd kept his as well.

Too soon to call? he wrote.

No, she wrote back. *But I have company right now.* Is that what Mig was?

Call you next week? he texted.

I'll call you. It would be easy to get together with Lonnie. Easy to talk to him. And easy enough to think she could fall in love with him. Couldn't she? Isn't that what her father had taught her? That you make a choice to love someone, every day, again, again.

Wind tossed some leaves from driveway to yard and back again. Suzette wondered if any pancakes remained inside, preserved in a glass container. Even cold, they would taste better than the ones she made, which often turned out tasteless or bitter, for she could never get any seemingly easy mix right.

She did not know what she would say to Mig, only that he was waiting.

Her mother would hate that Mig was there, would shake her head if she knew what Mig had said, how he had opened a door that Suzette had not realized existed. Flavia wouldn't like it either, but she would nod and ask Suzette what she pictured for her life. Her father would have told Suzette to walk toward the unknown, not to fear falling and failing, not to be afraid to live.

She thought of Lonnie and his love for her rugelach, and she considered backing out of her own driveway, showing up at Lonnie's door, but she stayed seated, as she often did when unsure. Behind the clouds that for so long had troubled the hemisphere, the belly of the sky was full of patient stars.

Suzette unbuckled herself from the car and got out. A bracing air pierced the night, like a sharp answer inhaled into a lung. She walked toward the house she had made into a home all by herself for her and Lena, and she thought of all the things she once thought she could never do, and how she had done them, and Suzette unlocked the front door, and stepped in.

Acknowledgments

Thank you to:

Erik Schwab, who answered a hundred grammar and punctuation questions with promptness and kindness and accuracy.

My cousins, Perla Miriam González Barreiro and Astrid Stella González Barreiro, who each helped me with Mexico-related facts and culture.

A bunch of people who helped me verify other facts: Courtney Pitre, Elizabeth Waugh-Duford, Janet Hawvermale, and many Facebook friends who readily chimed in to answer my questions about a bunch of stuff I did not know.

Elissa Schappell, who gave me feedback on some of this manuscript in its infant stage and whose lessons live on in my work.

Barbara Jones, one of the toughest critics I have ever had, but damn if I didn't come away as a better writer.

Fred Leebron, for taking a chance on my fiction.

Vick Mickunas, for all the support and for making me laugh on tough days.

All the journal/magazine editors who published my short stories. Every acceptance was a joy.

My blog and author newsletter subscribers, who help spur me on.

The Emporium in Yellow Springs, Ohio, where I wrote chunks of this manuscript over the years, sitting at my favorite table and drinking a cup of coffee. It's still my best place to write.

The many teachers at Antioch Writer's Workshop over the years. I was just one little person scribbling notes, but they were damn good notes. And to my AWW posse: Tina Neyer, Heide Aungst Manfredi, Leslie Pearce-Keating, and of course Melissa Fast.

Those who read the manuscript and gave me feedback, big and small.

Corinne Mahoney, who is still one of my most trusted editors after all these years.

The Book Cougars, Emily Fine and Chris Wolak, for taking time out of Book Expo to talk titles with me and for all the support, and especially to Em for being an early reader of pretty much everything and for telling it like it is.

All my text Queenies—Carla Sameth, Robert McCready, Liz Haberkorn, Pam Van Dyk, Andrew Rees, and Ms. M. Thank you for being a daily sounding board.

Courtney LeBlanc, who has taught me better how to champion other writers.

Jenny Robb, for listening to the play-by-play on weekday mornings.

My publisher, Kevin Morgan Watson, for believing in my book, and my editor, Claire Foxx, for putting up with me and my grammatical escapades.

Ranjit Rawlley, for cheering me on, and all my friends and other family members, including in-laws, who have championed my work.

My little family of origin—Hap, Sonia, and Romy Cawood—whose love and support always strengthens me. The best parts of me come from having grown up in the company of you three wonderful humans.

And last but never least, my husband, Preston McKee, for always understanding when I say, "I need to write now." Thank you for supporting my dreams and doing everything you can to make them come true. Most of all, thank you for being one of the dreams that came true.

Shuly Xóchitl Cawood grew up writing stories on her father's blue Selectric typewriter. She is the author of two other books: *The Going and Goodbye: A Memoir* (Platypus Press, 2017) and *52 Things I Wish I Could Have Told Myself When I Was 17* (Cimarron Books, 2018). She earned her MFA from Queens University of Charlotte, and her writing has been published in *Brevity, The Rumpus, Cider Press Review,* and others. Learn more at www.shulycawood.com